Steven Berkoff was born .... East End. He studied .... entered a series of reper .... he formed the London T........ professional production w........ *the Penal Colony*, an adaptation of one of Kafka's short stories. They presented his first original stage play, *East*, at the Edinburgh Festival in 1975. Since then Steven Berkoff has written, directed and toured with adaptations from Shakespeare, Edgar Allan Poe, Kafka and Oscar Wilde.

His plays have been widely translated and performed internationally and include: *Decadence, Greek, Harry's Christmas, Lunch, West, Acapulco, Kvetch, Sink the Belgrano* and *Massage*. *West, Harry's Christmas* and *Metamorphosis* have been adapted for television and were screened by Channel 4 and BBC2 in the early 1980s. Steven Berkoff has appeared in numerous films, and has recently directed his own film, *Decadence*, co-starring Joan Collins.

His published works include: *America*, a collection of poetry and prose; *A Prisoner of Rio*, a film journal; *I am Hamlet* and *Coriolanus in Deutschland*, both production diaries; and *The Theatre of Steven Berkoff*, a photographic history of his productions over the last two decades.

A number of stories from *Gross Intrusion and Other Stories* have been a source of inspiration for several one-man shows, including George Dillon's celebrated performance of *Hell, Say a Prayer For Me* and *Master of Café Society*. Steven Berkoff has himself performed *Actor*.

He lives in London.

STEVEN BERKOFF

GROSS INTRUSION

and other stories

Ω Quartet Books

Published in paperback in Great Britain by Quartet Books
Limited 1993
A member of the Namara Group
27/29 Goodge Street
London W1P 1FD

First published by John Calder (Publishers) Ltd in 1979

Say a Prayer for Me was first published in *New Writing and
Writers 13* in 1976

A catalogue record for this book is available from the British
Library

ISBN 0 7043 0196 2

Phototypeset by Intype, London
Printed and bound in Great Britain
by Cox & Wyman Ltd, Reading, Berkshire

Contents

Hell   1

Say a Prayer for Me   7

Master of Café Society   19

Actor   27

Daddy   32

After Joseph K   40

From My Point of View   51

Going Down   62

The Secret of Capitalism   67

Pictures   77

She or a Day in Brighton   81

Stardom   83

The Assless Dictator or
Homage to Miss Gascoigne   86

Gross Intrusion   89

False God   98

North   107

FOR SHELLEY

Hell

Sometimes I get so lonely. Like it's a disease you catch. And then I am alone. One day not having made some arrangement . . . forgetting . . . thinking that someone may call by chance . . . leaving it in fate's hand . . . so to speak . . . I find myself alone. It's terrible. It's not being alone. That can be good . . . but lonely . . . like everything's painful. Because you can't use your voice or your hands or your body. You can't use any of yourself and when that happens you have an ache . . . in your stomach, and you feel like a non-being. So since you can't speak. Hold. Make love. Dance. Play. You die. You drink. You smoke. You do anything to shut out the pain. I walk around the room. I turn on the TV, I see a wretched film. Wretched but I'm frightened to turn it off. And I have to keep smoking. Keep drinking to fill the hole of emptiness. I read sometimes but then the words start to dance and I get sleepy because reading's not what I need. I've read enough in my life. I want to live. And that is . . . hold a woman and love her. That's the best thing in the world. That's when I use everything at once. My words and ears and hands and body. And mind. And then I am transcended. I arise like the Phoenix Building Society out of the ashtray of my youth. Loneliness is a waste of time. Loneliness is a solitary profession. You can smell a lonely person. They stink of something that has an edge of fear to it. Like a plant not watered curls at the edges. A bit brown. But the horror of it is feeling like a non-being. When I'm lonely and sitting in my room I imagine myself as if from a great height ... a tiny figure alone in a tiny room in a tiny house. Just sitting there. Smoking and putting the kettle on again or sometimes abusing myself. That's awful. When there must be an equally lonely woman somewhere aching for an equally lonely man and I throw my love away. I toss it into the ash bin. I crush my love in Kleenex. And flush it down the loo ... and then I smoke. And then I turn on the TV and then I turn it off. And then I go to bed. And then I smoke in bed. And then I put it out. And then I look at my watch. Yes it is a respectable time to be in bed. It's not humiliatingly early. And then I put out the light. And then I curl up and then I hold my willy. Not for sex this time. But to cuddle part of me. A little part that's lonely. As if that thing was me. Sure I've tried to find someone to share this pool of loneliness. Sure I have. A hundred times. But they get out of the pool. Or we both get out. Or one of us gets bored. Because loneliness is a disease ... you have to give more to a person, a woman, than take me I'm lonely. After the sharing and the joy of finding someone and the knowing, there needs to be something else. I think so ... but each time it ends, the loneliness gets deeper ... it's like an acid and each time you go further into your shell to avoid it. You grow older. Less confident. You grow anxious. So who likes to meet ... somebody anxious ... so you smooth away the anx ... you smile and suggest a drive down to Brighton. Dinner. A movie ... a chat. An experience of

2

something. But your loneliness has bitten like acid into your soul. You can hear the acid sloshing around . . . a pool of loneliness. Inside. You try to love or make love. But love comes from joy. From excitement. What you give is not love but desperation to hold on to something warm. And each time it's an audition for the role of non-loneliness. So you invariably make a mess of it. Not just with her. With anyone. It's like a disease, you think there's maybe something wrong with you. You are prone to these attacks like having migraine or epilepsy. You wonder when the next attack will come. But it is more than that. It is a deep-down conviction that somewhere within you there is something . . . inferior . . . unworthy, and that exposure will lead to it being discovered. But 'tis loneliness that brings it on . . . this ugly feeling . . . and when it's there you're too lonely to do anything about it . . . to relieve it. So it's a circle. Vicious. The weekends and the nights are worse. Sometimes it feels like death. Since I don't feel alive. Being alive means living and feeling. Lonely means no one knows I'm alive except me and the cat . . . alone in my room. I can go out and sit in a café and people will mill around and that's comforting. For a while. I fill my mouth and fill my eyes with sights but when hunger is staved off . . . what then? I like the mornings 'cause I wake up and the day has not yet been etched in loneliness. I start with a fresh sheet. The same as everyone else. I'm hungry. I have things to do. Like put the kettle on. Go to work. But if I have no work then the day hangs over me like a threat that needs to be filled . . . especially on weekends. I look in my book for someone to ring. But usually it's too late . . . they're out or have arranged something. It wasn't always like this. Oh no. I used to sleep with a woman. The same one. I had a body to wrap myself around like a blanket. That's nice. You wake up with another human being. You walk down the street. You hold hands. You phone home if you're going to be late. You don't look in an address book wondering who to phone. You have that there that meets your need and her need. You don't look in books. I miss holding hands. I miss touching and kissing. I miss talking to her. Smelling her and making love. Then she went away. One day I came home and she had gone. I think she got bored. For me she was enough but she wanted some social life. I'm not so good at that. I like to stay in and cook a meal ... listen or watch a movie on TV, chat a while and go to bed. That's what I like doing. I find one person quite enough ... yes sometimes someone would visit. And then everyone would talk too loudly about everything that wasn't important and feel forced to have opinions about the food in Southern Mexico or the state of the nation and I couldn't get involved. So I'd talk less and less and eventually I'd shut up. And then they'd ask if I was all right ... like I was suffering because I couldn't vent some wisdom on some irrelevant matter and all I wanted to do was get them out so I could go to bed ... and cuddle my woman. The only good thing about those dinner parties was that they made the cuddle better by the sheer relief. I started to dread the next one. When the front door bell went I'd take a deep breath and put on a smile and pour out wine and smoke too much. But I don't do that any more. Cause she isn't here any more. One day I looked at a card in a window of a shop. Cards that lonely men look at. So I rang and went round. She was fat and awful. And the room was filthy. I went in

4

and the TV was on. It was eleven in the morning.
There were empty bottles and ashtrays everywhere. I couldn't think of entering her so I asked
for a wank. I sat on the sofa and took out the
thing which I had used in the past for loving my
woman. I took it out and she took it in one hand
and jerked away while watching TV. I shut my
eyes and pretended that it was OK but nothing
happened since it was too awful. I wondered
where I was to have come to this. This was love.
This was the fruit of my past. I've come to
collect . . . this . . . the sweet deserts of my life. I
paid her and went back to my room. The phone
looked at me like a dead thing and I smoked a
cigarette and sat in my room for a long time. Then
I went downstairs and fed the cat and stroked her
a few times. I then read all the letters I had from
my woman during the times we separated and
came together again. And then I looked at my
room and what I was in. A cell. The plates and
cups in the kitchen had piled up in the sink. The
laundry needed taking to the bagwash. There was
a fine from the library for books unreturned and
threat of court action. And a huge tax demand
brought about by neglecting my affairs. I looked
through the book for someone to ring and smoked
a cigarette but there was no one I really wanted
to be with except a woman or my woman. I didn't
just want to kill time. I didn't want to read and I
didn't want to watch TV. I didn't want to eat and
I didn't want to sit in the pub and get pissed since
all these were really ways of killing yourself. But
over a long period. That's when I thought that this
is really honestly worse than death. Much much
worse. This surely is living hell. And I wouldn't
expect it to change and someone to phone and
rescue me since I knew enough about habits

and patterns to see this as a recurring theme. And anyway it was raining and it always seemed to rain. I thought I could jump on a plane and go to Australia or America but the lonely habit would sooner or later return whether it was sunny, rainy, near or far. That's when I took the pills. There was nothing dramatic. I had some valium in the bathroom. About a hundred. I went out and bought a bottle of scotch. I took ten at a time with a swig and felt quite high and then I got violently sick but got over it and felt really good. I took the other fifty with water in case I got sick again. I took several hours to die since my life force must have really been quite strong and put up a hell of a struggle. I was not even discovered for four days since few people ever called round and the odd ring of the phone soon stopped. It was the bailiffs who had come to take my furniture for a debt who discovered me. I don't know how they got in. I watched the mortuary men move my body. They didn't know who to call since I had no living next of kin and didn't leave a note. And so they fumbled through my address book until they found someone who knew I had a brother I hadn't seen for years and didn't particularly like. There were few at the funeral. I felt very tranquil about the whole thing and could watch it all . . . like it was a dream. Although I did have a pang about the cat. I hoped the neighbours would look after it. They used to, when my woman and I went to Brighton for the weekend. Do you know I had that cat for fifteen years.

Do you think I'll be acceptable here being as it was self-inflicted. You see I'd quite like to meet some people.

Say a Prayer for Me

The manifestation of his lust was the salute to heaven by his obedient 'Lieutenant Flesh', whenever Doris genuflected with a bucket and brush and paid homage to the dirty floor with bubbly warm suds ... her generous ass rising and falling majestically as she pushed the brush forwards and backwards never failed to rouse the sweetest arias in the secret parts of Harry's anatomy and he would pause on the way to eggs and bacon floating in lavas of grease which fuelled him for yet another day in M. Burton's bespoke tailor and outfitter ... Doris's curly hair springing off the nape particularly attracted his base carnal throb, the sight of her white revealed flesh beneath the hair ... how the nape was a delicious ingot of pleasure ... that small rivulet and delicate avenue. But he never paused long enough to cough a word of carefully rehearsed, 'Hallo Dot, coming up to my room for a sensitive communication between two socialist vegetarians with sensualist leanings,' but such pithy utterances were not to drop from his anxious and mellifluous lips ... his passion was too strong and faltered, trembling against failure ... the endlessly long days in the store standing on his arches that were breaking under the dead weight that unrelieved boredom inflicts on a live body ... each evening washing the collar and cuffs of his shirt so that it should be dry for the following morning (possessing only two white shirts, the mandatory uniform made that little ritual necessary) or forgetting, he'd shrewdly put talcum powder on the collar and cuffs instead. This method though practical, caused quicker dirtying and faster fraying and consequently more frequent scrubbing. He would welcome the customers who were as confused about their clothes as he was about his whole life, hence they went to cheap multiple stores ... hoping to hide themselves in the wholesale taste of others, in the latest three button suit with insert pockets and Prince of Wales check, not varying too greatly from last year's model to cause any crisis of orientation. They sought in those infinite varieties of drab grey and lovat the answer to many puzzling features of their lives, most of all the key that would unlock their disturbing mediocrity ... the wife would stand in front of her man who suddenly became a sheepish object with no faculty of taste or choice ... suddenly was granted to the woman infallible depths of judgment and knowledge ... while the male seemingly had been made impotent by the metal edge of the tape measure stabbing his crutch. Unwholesome indignity 'would you please open your legs sir!' ... try desperately not to get too close and be made to feel their sagging equipment as his finger and thumb gingerly held the end of the metal extension. Harry, whilst dreaming about playing Petruchio or Richard II (out of work actor filling in as temporary labour) would reel at the stench, acrid ... bitter emanating from the evacuating areas of some Irish labourer or Indian who for indigenous reasons smelt somewhat higher than Harry and he would bite back the vomit in his throat ... during the long hours

8

in the shop, he mentally ran through all the plays he'd ever performed ... play over the good nights and gloss over the bad ones ... the bravos for one performance that he was so especially good in ... he played a weak snivelling psychopath and was thought good in the role but an actress who wasn't disposed towards him claimed that he was only playing himself, and advanced the same notion to the company who started to share her view when he failed miserably to make his mark in other roles. Only Harry was convinced that her judgment was untrue ... he was good in that role, the local critics said so; 'rare observation' they said. He liked that word 'rare', mulled over that review whenever he was depressed, it made him feel good ... so what, if he suffered the stinking effluvium of their dirty unbathed bodies, Harry was rare, and he would one day show them how rare he was ... he'd then remember all the directors he ever worked for, who for some reason never called him anymore ... his first nights and last ones and the little parties after in the dressing rooms ... the nights he'd sweat blood and fear and for no particular reason sail through on another night. The nights his friends came and chomped; his successes with his mouth in the bar warmed by the whisky that he also bought for everyone ... 'Well done Harry ... you were superb dear,' while he bought everyone's meal, just for liking him ... That was enough. I'll pay, I'm good. I'm up there on the green ... I got through another night in paroxysms of fear ... (secretly little spies in his subconscious delivered messages to him that he would try to reject ... messages that spelt fear, 'failure, forget your lines! You're a bum ... you're good ... sometimes but mostly you're a fake who's afraid of first nights

9

and throws them for the rest of the cast who bail you out' ... 'but I wasn't always like that,' he shrieks at those canny little spies ... 'your hair's getting thin' (true so I'll wear a toupé, so what, they're undetectable these days, my friend Bruce has got one, he can even swim in it) ... other times but usually not unconnected with alcohol ... 'you're a genius Harry, so observant, so "rare" ... so strong ... you're another Olivier' ... 'yes sir, three button and side vents' said Hamlet, Richard II ... Othello ... the fire in his soul that ignited those immortal creatures was crushed under the daily barrage of shit that stayed hard, constipated and adhered to the bowels of his spirit like concrete ... he could willingly tear the smug face off this or that man, could, 'tear him all to pieces, ... were every hair upon his head a life, there would not be enough to satisfy my revenge,' he'd misquote. The manager would watch him curiously, unaware of those monumental dramas raging inside Harry's skull. Like those people who with earphones are surrounded by a deafening cacophony revealing nothing to the onlooker except a distant glazed look, thus it was with H. The manager tolerated these temporary theatricals, but disliked them for their chameleon-like ease in changing lives ... for being able to essentially grasp in a week that which he had spent thirty boring, empty, fruitless wasted years doing, until the sacrifice of his youth was rewarded with the managership of a fading and ailing branch of M. Burton, a branch that even unbeknown to him was shortly to be lopped off at its withered stump with the manager still clinging to it while singing of the virtues of bespoke. To build up the importance of the trade to H the manager had alluded the complexities of the work. The difficulties of

10

measuring, the subtleties of serving ... nefarious
and discreet ways of licking asses and inducing
emotional blackmail by making the creeps buy
out of guilt ... buy what they couldn't afford ...
harassing the customers for your threadbare tot
of commission (these very methods had no doubt
led to the eventual cancer of that branch, since
word gets round in poor areas). 'Go forward No.
3,' the manager would bark as a pale innocent
customer would shabbily slink in. 'Yes, sir, what
can I do for you sir!' Harry would screech at some
nervous Cypriot, making an impression of rancid
keenness for the manager's watering thin stare.
'Forward No. 3.' H had metamorphosed from
'there cracks a noble heart' ... to sticky ...
unshaved ... chafed grubby talced cuffs, fallen
arches No. 3, with soiled underwear ... the direct
inheritance of being womanless and sapped of all
being, of all confidence ... all joy, no man but a
pest. A pest that needs to eat! A bug! Why live,
fool? Habit. He answered the question himself.
'Patch pockets, Donegal tweed, centre vent' ...
only for the freedom when he erupts from the
store like a fart. And he thinks of Doris, the scrubber in his digs, his bed and breakfast for working
men. Plump Doris bending to scrub the dusty torn
lino, the house cleaner. Nice Doris. The vision in
Harry's head, the 'perhaps this time I'll speak, if
she's washing in the kitchen.' He did. The day had
been too strong in horror and had seared open
some chemicals that had spelled a drop of courage
to his failing spirit. That night after washing his
collar and cuffs he came upon her on the stairs as
she was about to leave and inferred in jolly tones
all casual like with plenty of heart-thump how nice
to see her after hours so to speak to which she
easily and pleasantly accorded. 'That was easy,

11

what a surprise' ... she would pop in the next
night after supper (bed, breakfast and evening
meals), he shared a lodging house with other
lonely ageing unmarried men in an area of
London half way between hell and purgatory. In
the evenings they sat in a cold room watching
TV but knew, these womanless blokes, that the
flickering box of smiling-faced compères of quiz
shows and the like would only postpone the sense
of death which crept on them as surely com-
pounded by that box as by the dinner squirming
inside them which could only have been made
with indifference crossed with venom ... but this
night Harry would enter the Elysian Fields ...
would congress with Aphrodite and Juno, would
live for once ... she'll come up after she's washed
the supper dishes ... Oh fortunate hero ... servant of Priapus, upon thy white steed will he fly
far from M. Burton and No. 3, float serenely into
remote and profane regions of delirious escape ...
my angel Doris's ass leaping heavenward with her
pussy, Xmas wrapped in pink nylon (brief glimpses
last week), would sneak, ogre of wobbling carnal
appetites, into his room and be impaled by H.
He would live again, ... enter not Burton's, but
through his menacing, twitching, itching, pink,
stiff, arched cock that he would swift into her ...
into that steaming cauldron of Doris ... 'Oh hell
and fuck!' He sprinted upstairs to wash his equipment and waited with thumping ventricles, fag
choked ... minutes later ... a knock on his
door ... delicate ... like a whisper ... then came
an unwelcome visitor – fear ... 'Oh Christ', like
the fear of those first nights it entered even here
as if, starved of attention all this time, it had waited
for something important enough to Harry that
would swell his arteries with the blood needed for

12

a gesture of life ... the black phantom of fear descended greedily to syphon it off. 'Oh God' ... he feebly invoked ... he tried to smash it out of his skull but the images he had made of the future died ... the myriad paintings his skull had produced in its gallery faded as if washed with torrential rain. He opened the door with fear clinging to him still, like an invisible incubus fastened to his jugular vein. There she was ... cherubic with rosy rubric cheeks and glinting eyes ... she was wholesomely flushed with expectancy ... her *expectancy*. 'I can't stay long,' she smiled nervously ... while his salient or selling point was diminishing by the over-keenness of his love and the anticipation of her wants. His whorish picture of her genuflecting, 'easy grubby scrubber', was replaced by sturdy, strong, upright, made-up, expectant Doris ... she seemed to grow as he had been diminishing ... he satiated the porny area of his brain with a succession of tatty, threadbare pictures of her knees bent onto the mat and her creamy ass and dale to recoup the blood to that part nature demands for her deeds. But these days blood mostly rushed to his face in sweaty humiliation for his soul's sacrifice at Burton's and he cannot fuck with his face. And now again his face received the homage of blood that was meant for his prick. He wondered why and what had become of that bursting impatient tumescence that had twisted him up in desire until at last he had unfastened his strangled vocal chords to speak to her. She sat on the bed and he with fag relaxed just enough to act out a clumsy gesture of sexual greed. Sensed he an awful and sad need to prove his worth and her attractiveness, little knowing that she would have been just as happy for a chat ... to break the equally relentless monotony of her own plight ... her

13

threadbare daily existence with child at home, this unmarried gentle Doris saw in Harry a scintilla of sensitive being and hoped that what she believed she saw in him would also see the same in her. Might have detected in her the images of softness, homeliness, wifeliness and motherhood. Sure, he would understand her little two-year-old at home with mum . . . would like her, she hoped, smelling as she did of flour and fresh apples . . . she could look after him . . . Had seen and recognised the ravages of neglect that she was keen to mend. She had liked his voice (how the lonely look for virtues), a voice broader and different from the other tenants . . . gentle brown eyes. Thought that in him she would find the redemption she sought. Had her prayers eventually come true, that she uttered nightly to the blessed Holy Virgin . . . Had she in Harry, soft pliant baritone shy Harry, found the man she needed in her guts, to protect, comfort and sew for. She thought so . . . she needed to. She carefully made up and thought that even if he wanted to fuck her on the first night perhaps he would see her again . . . this one would, since she was afraid she lacked enough interest in her being to possess a man for long enough without succumbing to his blackmailing desire or anger if the passion she aroused was not immediately assuaged . . . so with Harry she was prepared to take this risk, just one more time . . . but trusting somehow in her prayers that he would succumb to the needs of real love and would be enchanted by her. And in this spirit thus she rapped on the door as gently as a caress; and thus in fear and self-loathing did Harry answer it. Fear bred from a fast depreciating assessment of his own worth. Doth reality ever live up to the private scenarios of hope? Not in Harry's case . . . it mustn't . . . it cannot be allowed to challenge those scenarios since that would be setting their dreams against the scope of his endeavour. And this endeavour was already weakened by fighting on other fronts. He grabs her in a rehearsed gesture which hurts her as much as it betrays him ... surely goodness and mercy is what is called for here ... stroke the curve of her cheek ... kiss the curls on her nape ... hold her palm in yours and confess in tears your frailty and beg absolution ... let the soul stride out of the body in all its lights ... ignite her spirit ... cradle her hopes like the Holy Ghost ... cry unto the Lord for thanks ... and render unto Caesar that which is Caesar's ... feel her heavy tears from the melting ice of anguish that you dissolve, feel them cascading down your face. And let the angels of libido feast only after the benedictions of Aphrodite ... sing Gloria and Kyrie Eleison ... 'the heavens break open' ... But Harry dimly aware of these injunctions to his soul pulled back ... smoked a fag which she shared and sent differing prayers to darker beings for the parole of his cock ... desperate transactions were going on at infernal depths whose conclusions were to be even greater fetters ... he relaxed a little ... not much ... enough to feed a kitten (the loan was coming through) a bare splinter of feeling threaded its bloody course and he fumbled with her clothes against her feeble cries and disappointments ... the devil flashed some tawdry pictures to enliven him ... just enough ... was made to think of her bending down humiliated and scrubbing, focusing on her innocent display of torn underwear ... Ah! Would this match with what he felt, what he could relate to, in fact to what *he* was. Was her sturdy uncompromising and hopeful glance as she entered the room too healthy for this withered plant. So he turned her over in imitation of those postcard pictures and attempted to fuck this creature who was just an article of flesh and clothing ... Faceless, in the sad poor furniture of his mind, pushed and heaved; her crying but yielding ... losing even now the gentle pictures she hitherto had formed ... losing them and fearing them lost for ever, while his deformed cartoons gained ascendancy ... yet the optimism that perpetuated the human race, that gives aid to the dying, that raises even that slashed wounded bull to its feet for its last futile clumsy charge, that will never say die even on the point of death, that will attempt to revoke the irrevocable ... inspired her sufficiently to hope that even after this initial degradation, born she thought out of a confusion of passion, frustration and filth would lead in a time of repose, to her cuddling him in her arms and forgiving him for being taken so cheaply. But now she couldn't even see his face but endured her wet cheeks on his rather grimy pillow ... during this onslaught, if it can be called that ... while Harry had taken a loan off Priapus against heavy interest (a further diminishing of his confidence) he hoped to fulfil his slender ambition of merely filling her space for the duration of time it takes to be a bedsitter hero. This was another night he would 'get through', not savour or enjoy but endure to the final act, when the audience would go to their homes forgetting in a short while that he had ever lived or breathed. Only the devil knew since the devil and its mate death feed upon a vacuum and lie in wait ... for them Harry and his like were important people that fed their monstrous and gloating appetites ... the strong only throw them crumbs but Harry donates his whole body ... even so

16

they were tiring of him ... Harry meanwhile was performing his ritual 'in and out', albeit a trifle limply but still at least making the gesture, when he started to think of the shop, perhaps seeing the shirt hanging over the chair as he was mounting her made a small mental reminder to him to wash the cuffs that night ... how the soul of man is distracted when not committed ... to think of the shirt cuffs *now* when inside poor Doris who was pushing her ample bum in the air to satisfy this beast's need to take his victims from behind ... OOOh! No! No! That shirt took his cock from his mind – that shirt hanging there like he was in it with its worn cuffs finally snuffed the hypocrisy that had filled his penis; that amazing construction of millions of years of evolutionary miracles had in Harry become uncertain, vulnerable. Not unquenchable, unbeatable, infallible as are nature's laws, but the appendage to his sense of failure. He failed Doris, he failed himself, and he failed God, he failed fate that had brought them together, and he failed her two-year-old that he surely would have loved, and his cock dismally fell out with a 'slurp' ... he mumbled something about 'being tired', 'sorry', 'not feeling too well' ... 'wonder what could be wrong?' ... Doris ... simple in understanding the jigsaws and circumambulations of human nature interpreted this in her own way – she was plain, not unwholesome, but not very attractive in the standard way of prettiness that men like ... not attractive enough even for a first fuck that she hoped might bring them to a closer union of heart, on her knees and elbows stimulating the morning's denigration with the evening's defilement. Both had souls that if united would have conquered everything ... worse ways, loneliness. After comes strength. Her baby needs a father ... this man needs her ... instead, her weeping, him angry and helpless staring at that shirt like some foul intruder had entered the room ... 'Who are you pale stranger? ... OUT!' he said to her ... 'Fine. Oh ... see you tomorrow' ... she said, 'sorry', she actually apologised (did crowds of angels sing her to her sleep?). The door closed gently and Harry went about scrubbing the sleeves of his shirt.

Master of Café Society

Up he would get as soon as dawn broke ... the day tracking over the slaty roofed house like cracked ice and glinting sprays and thin shafts of sun-white ... birds sang and sparrows crescendoed in triplets and arpeggios ... the sheets pulled back, feet out, toes wriggling, expectation rising, nose stuffed, phlegm sucked into the back of the throat, gathered into the mouth like a green harvest and then fed into a virgin Kleenex ... crushed, plop into basket. Outside engines beginning to throat up ... RARARARARARA ... Doors open and slam into the new dawn of life ... each new day indeed a miracle thawing out ... the world has made yet another revolution and still tracks through space holding a tight link to the everlasting sun whose gentle heat will not abide; the seas remain in the sea and do not flood the land; the nuclear devastation has not happened yet as promised, and no earthquakes disturb our shores. Revolution will not claim millions of lives here and we will not starve today, no fear of famine; the poles will not melt through overheating by an atmosphere already thickened with a layer of carbon monoxide that will act as a magnifying agent to the sun's rays, not today anyway. I will not die today of cancer nor be brutally stabbed in the throat by an irate black

19

panther choosing me to avenge some other deadly feud, no. So as the grey clouds stole across H's roof like a sargasso sea and as H carefully made his bachelor bed tucking in the coverlet, he prepared his mind to the joys of breakfast:-

The master of the working man's café society.

Steadfastly holding the same stretch of road each day, his perennial ritual (the same stomp down the road, so why don't you bloody say so), his eyes glazing already at the too familiar sight on the horizon blurring against the dreadful sameness, and wishing for fronds and palm trees and blistered chairs sun-baked and creaking under an Aegean sky, hot white islands, domestica wine and fat round sleepy tomatoes, but, as the unchanging sun rises with bloody and bulging cheek to penetrate the cool and fragrant mystery of dawn so doth rise Harry, phlegm-soaked and blinking, and as it sinks again with the dusk each evening without fail trailing garlands of purple glory, H will be there, wondering at the mystery of the universe as he contemplates yet another empty day ripped off the few petals of his life.

The image of breakfast floated before him like a menu visualised by computers and fed into his brain.

Hunger I like / it gives me a sense of purpose / for fuck's sake you can't live like this all your life / I eat to give myself a reason / I arise like all the other workers / buy a paper / sit down / they think I'm working / who else gets up to eat at 8 am looking tired / and yes I can see the real workers 'cause they're always talking about work / fuck it I work in my head / don't you stare at me like that in your

20

slave's uniform / your paint-splashed overalls / work doesn't grow on trees. MOTHER ... *some actors worse than you I've seen on TV. It makes me sick I mean with your looks like Paul Newman you look!!!!*

H had the same breakfast every morning. Why change? When he changed it confused him. It broke the perfect order of things. It took too long to decide whether one dish was better than another, since breakfast was the one special time of normality, getting up early, washing, being like all the other workers who were preparing themselves to enter the morning still freckled with white thick cups, sandwich toasted and packed full, eat slowly, let the first corner explode taste sensations in the mouth and hold back from rushing, because after this breakfast you are bequeathed purgatory, until once again hunger calibrates the day with purpose ...

H carefully opens the paper at the theatre reviews. Oh Ho! 'X's play is dull but sharp performances from the actors,' ... lousy actors always flog their mechanical characters on TV which buy up their little stockpile of samey parts, so and so plays such and such.

'We're looking for a statuesque young actress who can play between twenty and forty-five ...'

'Oh, I have just the person ...'

'Oh super ...'

'I don't like to offer it to you darling, since I wish it were bigger ...'

'Oh no, I'd really love to do it.'

'You are kind but do look at the script first and let me know.'

'OK darling but it looks fun.'

'Thought you were super last week in the final episode of *Justine* by the Marquis de Sade.'

'Gosh that was exhausting.'

'I can imagine ... bye bye ducky. I'll discuss money with your agent.'

CHORUS OF FAMILY: *These actors would convince the backside of my ass too good for them / Shmutters / No feeling / Not an ounce / 'Cause you're too good for them / Don't worry one day you'll show them / You'll have them licking your ... your agent doesn't ring you ... / So when are you going to get married / You're getting on for ... Soon you will be ... God don't tell me how old I am. I bury myself in the dustbin of wasted days and vomit my heart out and sit on the 73 bus sweating upstairs as the bus stands in the middle of Oxford Street and look how little I can do / And who lives for the sight of me / Gagged inside my raw mouth / I eat my failure like acid / Scorching / Hold back my tears ... and scorn my mother but I bite into her nipples withered and ancient as an old sack ... I bite into her ... take her by the throat and make her eyes bulge / After this I set her down gently and make a cup of tea / dad's watching TV all the time and didn't see a thing / He was stuck to the screen as a fly to paper / I will kill all the first-born theatrical agents /* DAD: *How come you don't get more TV /I saw a part you could have played on your head / Don't drink to get to sleep / Help! That's no good Harry ...* MUM: *My life you should have been a dancer so graceful you are ... Isn't he, dad ...* DAD: *What did you say?* MUM: *Graceful Harry is, I said he's so graceful that when he acts it's like watching a dancer, I said ...* DAD: *He's an actor not a dancer ... he acts like an actor / not a dancer /*

22

I opened his trousers ... I opened my father's trousers and saw his seventy-year-old penis and it resembled mine except his was only slightly withered / and pulled his Y-fronts down, old and faded but clean and dad said, 'Son you could be a good actor you're a professional / don't do it son' / but I took his withered old gentle cock in my hands and waited / I myself had made a journey through that very same place / mother smiling uncertainly as if trying to recall the time / we waited patiently and sure enough after a few minutes I detected a few thin strands of life stretching themselves out into affirmation / there's life in the old boy yet / well done dad / we all celebrated with a cup of tea.

Some cafés have a personality all of their own and H would sit in this one for the duration of the sandwich and order a second cup of tea ... Oh dear ... the sandwich has gone, diminished to a fast receding dream, it rests intestinally bright ... but the second cup of tea will start a second ritual ... a fresh cup ... we can begin all over again ... the workers graze past the windows and the cars form themselves into caterpillars. The traffic thickens and slows down and H can clearly see their eyes staring dumbly to the side from their fat satiated breakfasted faces. The snail's pace causes them insecurity and they no longer face the front, necessary with speed, since all they have to view is the standing back of another car. So they peer out of the corner of their eyes with a slothful curiosity, the way pigs raise their heads from the swill when disturbed ... the world that morning had been making itself into a stew and H sipped his second cup ... purpose would soon dry up with the absorption of it. He reads the

paper ... soaks up politics/theatre/ballet/history/
literature/sport/crime/sex/murder/tits/gags/gossip/
fashion/films/painting and nature ... and folds it
up ... it is nearly over ... the breakfast extinguished, the bed made, the walk achieved, the
selection of café decided on, the food ordered, the
table chosen ... the position of ass ascertained,
first tea drunk, sky surveyed and the wonders of
the universe wondered about, thoughts collected,
choice chosen, face shaved. There is no more,
an event that collects your life into a ritual
has come to an end: you could make another
ritual, but no. Hunger has been blunted ... the
body fuelled for work, attainment, achievement,
risk, effort, courage, daring, responsibility. You
stride out of the café ... alive ... paying the bill
with the certainty of a man about to embark on
the serious business of holding your fragment of
the world together ... the manager smiles at your
determined exit, admiring those secret events in
your life that make you an important personage
in his eyes.

*Your cousin Willy is so wealthy now ... / he runs a
Rolls-Royce / doing so well ... what did he do I ask
myself / he married well / of course he did / before that
he was nothing / Aunt Betty saw you the other night
on the telly / as the astronaut / I could tell it was you
in spite of the helmet / and she rang Willy to tell him
to watch it / you know, he's very fond of you / you
should go down and see him / but he wasn't in and
when she got back you were off the screen / what a
shame but she liked the bit she ... no your father
can't work anymore but we'll manage / don't you
worry / social security / so who's asking you for
money / when you've got it I know you'll give / I*

24

*know that / hold on a moment son your father wants
to talk to you / hallo son, I thought you did that part
smashin / you looked the image of Paul Newman
don't worry about money / listen I'd rather starve
alive with your mother and feed on rats than take
a penny from you that you might need for make-
up etc.*

H strolled down the street, his conscription with
the workers of the world was at an end, his brief
march with the hordes had come to a halt and
now he must turn back, no longer striding along
in the bright dewey sunlight with cloth cap and
sandwich box, ruddy cheeks, illumined with the
glow of purpose, tool-box gripped in the fist and
the thought of horizons to be conquered, wood
that needs to be shaped and hewn, metal smelted,
back bending under an easy load for a fit body
and a mate's rough voice shouting instructions . . .
no bricks to grip and chips to size, no plans to
pore over, no sweat to wipe from your brow, no
lunch break to look forward to, nor tea time
either, no home to rush home to, no dirt or grime
to wash off, no woman to say 'My god you're a
mess, what have you been doing Harry . . . jump
in the bath while I get your tea' / *like Paul Newman he
looks / with looks like that he could be. . . / your cousin
Willy is doing so well / your father wants a word with
you / don't worry son / Rome wasn't built in a day* . . .

Harry strolled down the street and opened his
familiar front door and re-entered his house as if
to say 'what am I doing here' . . . I should be
somewhere else . . . he sat down and felt like
crying . . . he sat in the chair and for the life of
him did not know what to do . . . so he did cry, he

25

cried like a man cries and to see a man cry is not an easy thing to witness, because a man will cry only when the end of the world has come . . . he stared out of his swollen eyes when the thought hit him . . . 'Fuck it, I forgot to get the cat food.'

Actor

Greetings, hallo John, hallo Richard, and how are you/hallo Mike/how are you/working/really that's good/what are you doing/a play/how really fine/ see you/have a nice day/hallo Peter how are you/ I'm doing well too/working/you are/that's good/ bastard he couldn't act his way out of a paper bag/ the slag/still I'll show them/those out there/the faceless ones/the ones in the chairs/they haven't the guts to get out there/hallo darling/you're lovely/you really are/I think our fate's designed in the stars/you're divine/yes I do really take this woman to be really mine/get the kettle on love/ it's nearly nine/hallo Ma this is . . ./going just great/ getting on fine/just watch this space/'So why couldn't they get you a commercial or two'/sorry ma/that's not what I have in view/for me/that's for the others/not men of quality/'I saw you last week on the TV/an astronaut/but couldn't see your face/ I rang aunty Betty/she raced for the set but when she got there/it was off the air'/bye ma/yes darling of course I'm as happy/how can you doubt/I haven't kissed you in weeks?/sometimes you forget/stop nagging I'm trying to work on my text/ if I don't work soon/I don't exist/that's a feeling these days that tends to persist/hallo John/how are you/you working/oh/I'm glad that you're pulling through/I'm glad to hear that all your efforts are

27

beginning to bear/fruit/is that the word/Fred how
are you/you working for TV/directing oh that's
cool/then don't forget me/ha ha ha/your old chum
from school/how did he/he flogged his bum/suc-
ceed/that weed/joined the club/the faceless ones/
all rub shoulders in the bar/the ones who can't do
it/the ones in the chairs/the ones who say thank-
you and who's next/hallo darling/had a nice day/
yeah I did nothing/walked streets and sat in cafés/
get a job/I'm an actor you bitch/got to be free/got
to be fit/no one phoned/are you sure/you were all
day/at home/hallo John/you working/you are that's
good/you'll go far/acts like wood/hallo Jack/what's
new/nothing aah tough/things will improve/the
going is rough/remember at RADA what they
said my dear/if you want to be a star you have to
persevere/if you want to be top of the shit heap/
you mustn't complain/if your shoes stink of turds
at the end of the day/hallo darling/what's your name/
you're lovely you are/I love you forever/you're
what I'm looking for/you keep the TV/I'll keep
the car/we'll sell the house/can't stand no more/
hallo Joe/I'm doing great/up for a series/not yet/
short list/near as damn it/I'll get you a guest/
spot/if you like/my agent's talking money/then it's
sewn up/hallo darling, sure I love you/hold on
there's the phone/did I?/no/sure there'll be other
parts/the bastards don't give me the shit from their
ass/hallo ma/hallo pa/how are things/I've seen
nothing but rubbish on the TV/why aren't you
there son/you look like Paul Newman/doesn't he
dear/hallo dad/don't talk to me you parasite/you
bum/all you can do is scrounge when you come/
yeah! I'll be keeping you one day/you old cunt/
don't talk to your father like that/be a son/that we
can be proud of/whenever we speak/I've got an
audition/I swear next week/to be/or not to be that

is the question whether 'tis nobler in the mind/to bear the slings and arrows of outrageous fortune/ thank you that's enough/we'll let you know/ we'll contact your agent/please don't phone/yes darling/it was great/the money will flow/so what I've not made love in a month/what's in your head romance and bullshit that's for the dead/ then go/fuck off/sorry I wed/you/hallo Richard/you doing well/you doing a movie/fucking hell/no!/ that's smart/you've got a good agent/mine's just a fart/anything going/any more parts/that require my stunning talent/oh, it's all cast/bastard/wouldn't give you the shit from his ass/hallo did I get the job/didn't think I was right/cunts/I could act the pants off the slobs/theatre/it's full of the dead/ they rake the graveyards/the lousy shitheads/their walking corpses/little blind mice/rats in armchairs/ hallo she hung up/hallo darling I'm back home/ dear John/sorry I really must go/sorry to leave like this/I just got so/bored with the life/ bored with the fight that must go on/day and night/ don't forget to feed pussy/please don't write/I'll find better than you/go/I don't care/you got no guts/I won't shed a tear/hallo John how are you working/ no/good/I mean good you're not dead/it's good that you/hold on/hold on to your soul/or take arms against a sea of troubles and by opposing end them/to die to sleep no more and by a sleep to say we end the heartache/thank you we'll let you know/and please/we do ask you not to phone/do I have a chance/tell me/you can tell me now/if I'm not the right one/then I'd/we're thinking about it/ call in the next/hallo ma/hallo pa/no I got no dough/lend me a fiver just to get through/I need a few bob/times will improve/'He looks like Paul Newman doesn't he Al?'/'He looks like a ponce'/ go to hell/I'll show them/I will/I'll smash through/

I'll show them what talent is/I'll break fucking
through/hallo darling/you're lovely/you look like a
peach/you're really divine/any commercials even/
will you be mine/my wife ran off with the telephone line/there must be something/I think we're
made for each other/like fate/no I don't exude
hate/I love the bastards/I'm all sweet and charm/
all right I'll lick ass/all greasy and smarm/she hung
up/hallo John/you working/you are/where/show me/
I'll be a star/yet/fuck you/you pigs/you bare your
asses/you untalented shits/shit gathered together
in one bowl/I'll flush you away/give me a role/
what do you mean cancer/yeah I'll try and get
round/yeah that word has a ugly sound/who would
fardels bear to grunt and sweat under a weary
life but that the fear of something after death/
hallo darling I love you! Oh leave me alone/
I've got other problems/so fuck off just go/you fed
up with me/women like you they grow on/ma
don't die/don't go just yet/don't leave me just now/
I'm starring in/*Hamlet*/I think/you'll be proud/
what did she say/her last words/'fore she passed
away/You look like Paul Newman and have a nice
day/goodbye ma and pa/I'll cry at your grave/but
I've got an audition I mustn't be late/whether it is
nobler in the mind to suffer the slings and arrows
of outrageous fortune thank you very much/we'll
let you know/please call your agent/please don't
phone/hallo/did they want/no/why/I have to know/
get the fucking kid out of here/I'm on the phone/
she hung up again/oh no/hallo John/what's new/
how's tricks/yeah terrific/I do bits/and pieces/maybe
Hamlet/too old/I'm an actor you prick/hallo
darling I'm home/what's this/couldn't stand any
more/don't be upset husband/don't be sore/just
couldn't stand it any more/need peace for the kids/
you can see them of course/say once a month/ we'll

discuss it in court/get a job and I'm sure you'll find/at the end/peace of mind/you mad/I'm tough/ the others are assholes and creeps/pigs at a trough/ halloJack/halloFrank/how'sgraft/readyourreviews/ you're doing good/you're smart/a good agent/that gives you the start/yeah I'm great/got to fly/mustn't be late/to be or not to be that is the question/ whether 'tis nobler in the mind to bear the slings and arrows of outrageous fortune/outrageous fortune/ to die/to sleep/no more and by a sleep to say we end the heart/ache . . . . ma!

Daddy

The steam was rising furiously in clouds that
obscured the other bodies in the room. He was
watching the figures move in and out of focus
like ghosts ... the sweat oozed gratefully down
his body and over his eyes and trickled into his
mouth ... every pore became an exit for the dirt
and grime that was locked inside his skin ... the
heat moved everything, shifted and broke up dirt
into valleys and streams, and he rubbed his legs
and belly satisfied ... it rolled off in shreds of
dead matter ... he was cleaning ... burning up in
a slow lather of sweat ... his head rested on a
wooden curved block, and the thin apron they
issued at the reception lay like a wet Greek toga
barely covering over the erogenous zone ... so
carefully placed as to reveal to inquisitive bulging
eyes the faintest rotunda of an aware prick ... not
stiff yet ... but just lolling expectantly ... a dark
shadow in his groin within which fantasies danced
and formed mirages in the heads of the old queens
that sat close by or walked casually up and
down ... they walked as if garlanded in chiffon
gowns carrying steaming trains which dissolved
behind them ... only the hissing of the vapour
and the occasional slap as flesh massaged itself,
morse-coding its proximity to the other occupants,
were to be heard ... the rest was heavy and

32

expectant silence . . . it was hot, becoming unbearable if one moved . . . the air scorched into the
lungs and hurt. 'I could leave,' thought Cyril 'and
take a plunge – icy-cool – and return', but just as
he was thinking this he became aware of figures
rising and sinking . . . one or two leaving . . . the
patterns in the steam creating new configurations
and swirls as the doors opened and shut . . . if the
door to the outer room stayed shut for a while
the steam's thickening camouflage would prevent
snooping eyes from detecting what two intense
and barely moving figures were doing in the
corner . . . would only just make out a shape and
then one has at least eight to ten feet warning
to recover the apron and conceal the monstrous
swelling before the eyes came too near . . . each
figure feared the others as if convinced of the
solitariness of their deviation . . . scarcely crediting
the moving misty creatures with desires as strange
as their own . . . the separate race, inured and con-
ditioned as odd . . . from the early days when the
desire to be a woman and want other men was a
dirty criminal passion . . . so this fear grew into
alert caution, even though the occupants of the
steam rooms were of a feather . . . this fear to be
caught in the centre of one's shame, thrown out, or
just ashamed of their dirty itch . . . like schoolboys
jerking each other off in the lav, mustn't be caught
by teacher . . . and yet fear breeds a stranger thrill
at the same time . . . to be seen in the heat of one's
delight, in the daring exposing of one's secret
fantasies . . . no one knows . . . no one, not one's
closest friend, wife, family, not in there, in the
sanctuary of heat and steam . . . one is depersonal-
ised into mere hard warm pliant flesh . . . naked
and nameless, no names given . . . not even
speaking . . . that is part of the ritual of sacrifice . . .

the knowledge of the name, the timbre of the
voice which would identify or code the speaker
would make it impossible ... would reveal a
conscious act ... so no. I have left my body ... it
does things that the owner of a voice would never
do ... only unguarded blood-filled and aching
flesh making its own demands, being the king for
the day ... just the nervous eyes peering ... the
hand moves in slow motion, its fingers, white
tarantula ... crawling nearer and nearer the
source of blood-boiled lust, they halt nervously ...
signal caught by victim whose knees crook casually 'accidentally' apart ... reveal the blood-filled
prey ... a tumescent lump of flesh ... the hand
now moves like clawed hunger and seizes the
offering between finger and thumb ... starts to
press, squeeze, rub up and down slowly, gently,
with the confidence of one who knows that
ensnared in its grasp is an animal that cannot
escape, entrapped in the prison of its own terrible
desire whose only freedom lies in the power of the
unknown manipulator ... the freedom will come
when his prick will grow so huge that he will be
able to crawl through its centre ... when his body
will simply leave and turn to lava ... will throb
his thick white swill and he will escape ... escape,
metamorphosed into a pool of spunk that will be
washed away along with the collected sweat and
dirt and other emissions of the baths ... shadows
come and go ... the hand stops on occasion (an
alert hind sniffing danger?), figures dissolve themselves in the swirling mists like beings brought to
life for a few seconds and then returned to the
incorporate air ... the hand continues ... wanking
as only a man knows how to wank another man ...
with the specific and ancient knowledge of the
flash points in that stiff and bursting cock, able

like a guided missile to home in on the areas the wanker knows so well. Searching the rills and ridges, the exact amount of pressure ... the time when speed takes one into incredible flights into the stratosphere ... not too soon ... don't spend too fast ... the recomposing shapes in the mist provide insurance against over-eagerness ... the strange warm satisfaction of a man's fist, heavy, large, seeking out one's shame ... that's what so good about it ... so secretive ... not open, accepted naturally ... meet the folds ... but mysterious ... dirty ... unaccepted ... even by oneself in the cold light of day ... there, clothes describe the owner's taste, class, personality ... too much given away, too much to risk ... only in the steam room protected by the blankets of mist rising and the neutral anonymity of nakedness can you surrender to the full, the implications and impulses the clothed conscious daylight being would reject ... except ... the memory of some fleeting, hurried experiences in cinemas protected by noise and darkness. His teenage was scored by several such events (perhaps the birthplace of his corruption and subsequent desire for darkness and secrecy), as if sewn into his unconscious was the knowledge that male desire and furtiveness were immutable ... the image of his wet prick spraying his pants ... his heavy breathing ... the awkwardness of not being able to stretch his legs or open them to release his high young fulsome jets ... no, here was better ... one can wash the spunk away in the shower ... in the plunge ... wash away the guilt ... not face the brilliant light of day after the cinema's damp sticky gropings ... no words exchanged ... just let the hand ... strong heavy masculine hand work its joys ... and let one's body melt away into the steam ... into the water ...

35

into the drains ... feeling that, he relaxed, and waited ... sensing a shape through the mist that grew larger ... he closed his eyes, partially surrendered like a woman. That's what was so burningly satisfying, being the object of lust, his wife could never do that for him; make him feel ... coy ... he withdrew a knee ... make him work for it ... he could act a woman so well ... as a child he fantasised about being a girl, who was fucked so hard by so many men ... images occurred of sucking so many juicy hard pricks ... as a girl he did not imagine that he could exercise the restraint that women seem able to assume ... even when he eventually fucked them ... from where, he often wondered, grew this strange flower of his desire ... the offshoot from his natural fucking male self, often called a womaniser, a ladies' man, a Don Juan ... where developed this curious thing that grew like a small delicate unknown ... unclassified plant within his psyche ... blossoming in those special seasons within the body and spreading its noxious fragrant scent through his senses which did not resist but simply and casually obeyed its strange demands ... and that particular afternoon taking time off to feed this flower in the Turkish baths ... no one knew, or even hazarded the vaguest guess ... mother ... wife ... father ... no, not him, though from him he sensed the greatest fear ... the greatest censure of any fault he harboured ... his father was the governor of a prison and he the prisoner having to answer for all his sins which seemed engraved on his forehead. Upright, righteous father ... he even felt guilty standing before him as if his desire might be writ in letters of fire ... these thoughts flew between him and his blood and drained some stiffness from

36

his member but he immediately washed them away . . . the heat made his mind swim . . . its power melted away any distasteful images before they could coagulate in his mind . . . it purged and purified until all that was left was body . . . naked relaxed and expectant body . . . the air scorched into his lungs like sulphur . . . he could only endure it a few moments more . . . the figure grew out of the mist and sat near him . . . its intention seemed plain . . . he dimly saw an arm stealing towards him and he lay back like a cat ready to be stroked . . . from a lying down position he need only encounter the hand and could keep an eye on the door . . . the strategy was familiar to all . . . the stranger's hand found him . . . found his flesh . . . primed and ready . . . and the stranger wanted only his hand and eye to be fed by the younger man's prick . . . relinquishing his gaze only to keep surveillance on the door . . . if a shadow seemed in that faded moist jungle to linger, attracted by the composition of two still bodies . . . the secrets they might harbour . . . the stranger's hand would stop, then return, adding by its absence a sharper awareness . . . what a strong hand . . . how well it sensed the rhythm of his body . . . like an organist pulling out the right stops . . . fantasies crawled through his eyes and dissolved into a myriad of liquid shapes . . . the sperm felt like it was boiling . . . the stranger's frenzied strokes slowed suddenly . . . not wishing his quarry to escape until he lowered his head to receive the warm homage in his mouth . . . dangerous, if someone came in the door . . . the act of recovery to upright position would reveal their game . . . would be too violent a gesture . . . the spunk ready to emit at this point held back, reined in by this sudden conscious act of defence . . . the

body wanted now too much ... too much to care
for caution ... the sap was rising on its carefree
abandoned voyage to ecstasy ... let him, it will be
over soon ... surrender to it ... the stranger
leaned over ... this thinning hair revealed a shiny
sweaty dome which further decelerated the
onslaught to come ... he didn't wish to see him
so clearly ... older than he liked, even though he
did like older men ... this one seemed too old ...
if he sucked hard he may reverse the slowing
process ... the older man looked up as if to query
humbly the almost imperceptible, but certainly
softening growth in his mouth ... THEIR EYES
FOR ONE SECOND IN THAT CHAMBER OF
HELL LOCKED ... the mist cleared enough to
show ... something ... He was in a dream ...
knew he was trapped in a nightmare and struggled
to free himself from it ... knew certainly that this
nightmare would go, too incredible ... too
horrible ... must go ... but his flesh was real ...
the marble slab in the room was real ... the heat
was real ... the sudden release of the stranger's
hand was real ... the standing up and rushing out
of the room was also real ... as he pounded up
the stairs, and even without showering dressed,
still sweating furiously ... out in the cold air ...
still sweating even more now than in that
inferno ... he swore to himself that the face of his
father that lowered itself on to his cock, was a
manifestation of his guilt ... a vision of fear that
harboured itself in his brain ... a revenge on his
split mind ... the flower seeking to dominate
his being ... but the balding head, those eyes, the
white face that seemed to twist itself into a question mark of horror ... so real, scored itself into
his mind like a cauterizing iron ... he was not,
since he hurried away, in time to witness the

stranger several minutes later leaving the same establishment at a rhythm which was not usual among the clients who had sweated and relaxed for two hours . . . more the pace of a criminal in a city full of police.

After Joseph K

Harry entered the stainless steel and chrome rein-
forced-concrete gallery whose façade had been
stressed against wood, hence a textured look. It
was, as is normal in galleries, white . . . and marble
floored, with schemes of white arteries running
through. To step in here was holy, it had the
cool silent atmosphere of churches . . . the air was
filtered through an electro-gauze mesh that filtered
out any impurities and regulated the temperature.
The pictures were uncrowded and occupied space
that was comfortable . . . In the centre of the
room on what appeared to be an onyx dais and
lit from above in a circle of blue light was a
man kneeling and resting one hand (his right)
behind him. In front of him, just obscured by
some spectators (H walked round), there
was also a kneeling figure, crouched, of a woman
with flaring red hair and cerulean blue dyed
skin, vermillion nails and mouth. She was
crouched over in an attitude of prayer and then
Harry realised that the combination of the two
bodies was deliberate and that the woman was in
fact sucking the man's penis . . . her head movements were steady and unhurried and the man
was equally undisturbed. The exhibition was
partly devoted to conceptual art which had eluded
Harry's interpretation but drew his curiosity. H

wondered to what extent familiarity had inured the couple to celebrate or enact this piece of conceptual art, and made graven images in his skull of delights forbidden to him in the freer air that they breathed. He tried not to be aroused by the spectacle but take it casually as the other spectators seemed to be doing . . . although he did notice one silver-haired man smirking in a knowing way as if totally unruffled . . . 'Oh we know who you're fooling,' his bronzed winter tan seemed to be saying and Harry smiled back at him . . . 'Yes, I too get the jest,' but the man had missed (intentionally?) the trajectory of Harry's smile which flew off into space and then shrivelled not being fed, and the tan let his own knowing smile fall onto a very pretty young woman who had a hold of his arm in a protective or proprietorial way which sent a filament of sickness into Harry's craw at the thought of the time that had passed since he last crooked his arm for a woman. The two now looked at each other in a way that spelt an infinity of secrets, disregarding the naked couple, or perhaps, reminded so strongly of their own closed doors that they became lost in a reverie . . . She looked too clever for Harry anyway . . . too knowing . . . clever women he couldn't abide, he preferred intuitive sluts or bright Monroes. But intellectuals – Oh dear no! The posed man and woman suddenly struck him as a parody of Rodin's 'The Lovers' . . . the woman was resting now and smiling quite gently as if the effort though not tiring was nevertheless demanding, as a pose essentially must be, and some of the audience smiled back with her in empathy and not a little admiration, as if she was proving something to all womankind, some inalienable truth that her courage was liberating for them. The man meanwhile had redistributed his weight to the other arm but since he didn't smile at the audience they didn't smile back at him. Her cheek was resting against his knob ... still quite firm, 'amazing,' H thought, and she looked as if she might have been holding a carnation to her cheek ... obviously this can't go on all day ... could it? Perhaps they take a break for tea and return ... He looked for a title which rested on the plinth, one of those wooden triangles such as are used by bank tellers and it said simply ... 'The Circle Line Shall Survive' ... curious title and it left no association or reference that he could immediately discover to make the event any easier for him to understand. By now more people had filtered through past the doorman, looking resplendent in a navy serge uniform and gold buckle and glowing red cheeks such as seamen have who when retiring after long years at sea take jobs as porters ... but it's always their roseate glow that betrays their origins. Harry was tempted to test his little theory on the porter, anticipating the porter's chuffing guffaw of delight at the correct diagnosis, but the porter was far too busy searching people's bags since the provocative nature of the exhibition might tempt an unbalanced vandal or even worse. The girl had now resumed and lifted the man's rather sagging penis into her mouth which simply fell out lacking, after this interval, the impetus to keep it there ... the spongy tissue, glands and muscle had collapsed, no doubt caused by an exhausting day, naturally more so for the man, biologically, in sustained concentration whereas the woman's effort was purely physical. As it dropped out a second time a couple of suppressed giggles came from the audience. One girl with cropped hair and prominent teeth had turned her

back on the proceedings and had stuffed a
handkerchief in her mouth to suppress a gale of
laughter which otherwise might have exploded out
of her. The gentle giggles nevertheless echoed
around the gallery's vast spaces . . . one man was
concentrating very hard, he had long hair and
dangling at his hips was a Nikon camera with a
200 ML lens and the other appurtenances owned
by serious photographers. H had once longed to
study photography and possess a camera but
somehow his career as a comedian, though not
booming, made demands on his time . . . even
when not working, routines must be polished up,
new gags learned and tried out, and his success
such as it was (he had worked for six out of forty
weeks this year), was not royal but reasonable . . .
it kept him on his toes. He must be ready when
the time comes and not be found out of condition.
That would be fatal. Sharp and ready, not for
the pubs and working men's clubs but the smart
restaurants where they have silver service and the
night clubs, music halls and even the theatres . . .
a friend of his once had two years
in a West End run . . . Two years! Continual
employment . . . He ran over the word 'two' as if
he could savour the taste of it . . . his agent realised
his gifts . . . that's good . . . The male model by this
time had recovered his aspiration sufficiently to
hold it firmly in her mouth and the woman whose
hair fell over the 'sight' in a great cascade, combed
her finger through it, with a gesture of unveiling
it from time to time, but it kept falling back in a
waterfall of riot red . . . blood red, he conjectured
evenly. Now H was beginning to feel murmurs
of appreciation within his groin . . . he identified
himself in the role . . . could he do this, would he
ever even take his trousers off in public, he winced

visibly at the idea, a picture which occasionally
manifested itself in the most acutely embarrassing
dreams. He idly wondered if the man had already
come or was planning it later or had not come
and would not, so as to better preserve his act
or exhibition ... He must really be tired but the
definition of his triceps convinced H that his condition would enable him to sustain that position
on his elbow for an unlimited time. H seldom went
to galleries but this Sunday and for no particular
reason he was tempted by the sound of an exhibition of European Conceptual Art and took the
172 bus, partly out of curiosity, partly to escape
from the deadly boredom on a Sunday afternoon
sitting in his gardenless flat where only his mother
kept a watchful eye. On a sunny day, particularly
on Sundays, the claustrophobia of the flat would
intensify and his ageing mother (he must get his
own flat one day, just give me twenty consecutive
weeks of work! ...) would sit in a vague stupor
reading the *Sunday Mirror* or the *Sunday People*
and say, 'Why don't you go out Harry, you're miss-
ing the sun ... where's Micky, how come you don't
see him no more? ... or Betty?' ... he hadn't seen
this girl Betty for years but in the confusion of
her sense of time the years somehow all merged
into each other whenever she tried to recall an
incident. He hated her suggestions which although
well meant contained an implication of loneliness
merely by implying that he had lots of friends ...
his brows creased and the skin on his scalp
tightened ... unpleasant flat, with his old room
since childhood ... he once moved out and was in
demand in the small provincial towns as a quick
likeable comic, whose jokes though not always
up to date still had an innocent charm about
them, derived from his awkward rendering of old

44

favourites. He was attractive then, with curly hair and brown clear eyes ... but his hair had thinned and his eyes become a trifle bloodshot ... the rending of his attributes left him no cover for an awkward delivery, which though once charming was now stale. Work lessened, and he moved back home temporarily, tried out new material in the kitchen using his father as a guinea pig. His dad always laughed at his gags which relaxed H enough to be really funny, since the essence of a good comic is not so much his material but his delivery. But the audience was not his dad and in the silence of the response he would tighten up and revive his old awkwardness. During his brief return home his father died of cancer which made moving out rather more difficult until he had gained sufficient work to run two homes ... which he would do in time! 'Struggle maketh man!' he propounded, loudly enough to be heard ... he fed himself these little homilies from time to time, usually when under stress. The gallery was a peccadillo or chance whim. He knew galleries to be haunted by women, particularly foreign students who would skim around armed with a notebook ... He had had two such affairs from his gallery sojourns which were mercifully brief, since he held out no interest for them after an initial sortie into his personality, and neither they for him. All he wanted was relief; one, as a receptacle for his semen and two, a crack at loneliness. He would have liked the affairs to have lasted but saw no future for a foreign girl in his life. One girl he did bring home to meet his mother, and his mother had fallen asleep in front of the electric fire with her legs apart and was snoring loudly ... Harry took the girl into his room where they played some of Ravel's music and the golden

45

oldies selection on the gramaphone, and in spite
of his unwritten rule never to make it at home, was
so tempted. Whether this was through boredom or
lust or merely to do something that might render
the evening memorable in some way for both of
them, he could never be sure. As the fates would
have it mother wakes up *now* when she should be
sleeping ... she came in to say goodnight and was
in time to witness H's mauve protuberance steaming in and out of the Dutch girl's embarrassed
ass ... a spectacle surely full of horror for all
three participants, and the outcome of the affair
was to make the mother ashamed and Harry
disgusted with his own flesh and resolved never
to bring a woman home again. He had broken
the sacred biblical injunction, 'Do not uncover
the nakedness of the son to his mother', even
if unintentionally ... his mother (Oh no!) had had
the sight of his monstrous lust, the thing most
profane and secret in the strange relationship
between mother and son, his erective potential,
seen there glowing in all its rampant glory. Innocent mother, enters with flush and patchwork legs
from electric fire to apologise for falling asleep,
exits with face as pale as dad's deathmask. These
thoughts cluttered and brayed in his skull as if to
punish him for neglecting them, whereby their
invocation may in some way point to a moral
lesson. He was then attracted to another exhibit,
in fact only just noticed it tucked as it was in the
corner of the gallery. It was of two people sitting
at a table eating a chicken, which they picked at
very gently and ate slowly since they must be there
all day. There were less people surrounding this
exhibit ... H almost preferred this one since he
didn't wish to seem fascinated by lingering too
long at the previous exhibit lest his motives

appeared more base than aesthetic. The eating was fascinating and it surprised H how interesting such a simple daily event could be ... I mean ... you do see it every day ... like at restaurants and at home with his mother ... 'would people queue to see me eat with her?' ... 'watch her put her teeth in folks. Oh! Now she's taking them out again.' The idea raised a dull pebble of laughter in his aching gut. The man and woman eating (male and female again, perhaps some link here) seemed very happy and would make appreciative gurgles and moans of delight and in between mouthfuls would say some words and then repeat the dialogue all over again ... so obviously they were not making it up ... How curious that by putting them on a plinth, they became an exhibit. Harry is an exhibit. He thought of the small stages in the Saturday night pubs with bad mikes that couldn't convey his jokes properly because of static, of the waxen droop of boredom that afflicted the customers like the plague ... of his sickening loss of his sense of being ... *even alive*, and why. Of his agent sitting watching him when there were only ten people in the house, and no one laughed, no one except one senile old lady who was unbalanced anyway and giggled for no reason and in all the wrong places as if afflicted by some private pantomime in her head, or per-haps the sight of a man standing on a small platform gently lathered in grease which plopped on the floor and wearing the gibbering grin of an idiot was a subject for uncontrollable mirth. No doubt it was. Agent spat, 'audiences are shy to laugh when there are so few people in the house, you know that son.' The couple eating continued chatting ... starting the loop again. He liked the way they spoke and were so utterly involved in

each other's actions. Pouring out water for each
other... 'pass the salt and pepper would you
dear,' completely oblivious of anyone else around
them... even if H was only two feet away they
seemed totally unaware of his existence. He
thought that if he touched them like you might
touch a statue they wouldn't notice... would be
completely impervious to him and he was
tempted, was on the verge... 'Hell, they're in
showbusiness like me,'... could I be so oblivious,
he thought... imperturbable, untouched in this
white gleaming and antiseptic gallery... neon
struck... could I get on stage and be that 'cold'.
Yes, that's it. He hit his brain with the word as if
assuming that this new knowledge that the event
had imparted to him could easily be transplanted
onto him, and acted on that swiftly merely by the
discovery of it... 'an insight to heaven'. He still
wanted to touch the hand of the woman that now
rested casually on the table... just to test his
theory... there he was, heart pounding as it never
did before, as if to meet the challenge that would
change once and for all the course of his life...
what could she do... she couldn't kill him...
certainly wouldn't shout or scream. He stood in
the middle of the universe of his thought, caught
at a moment of a momentous decision... his
mother was at that very moment, unknown to him,
weeping in her small, neglected and rather smelly
flat... weeping for him, for the son that she had
hopes for, not for herself but for him... 'just some
pleasure out of his life' and prayed every night for
his success and a nice girl... that they could live
there for a short time until they found a flat...
they could even have her room. What did she
need with a big bed now that the being who had
made that amount of space necessary and had so

amply and warmly filled it was gone out of her life
forever . . . the space even tormented her, filled as
it was with the years of his soft breath on her back
and his heavy arm over her shoulders . . . so, she
conjectured, Harry and 'her', whoever that 'her'
was going to be, would have the big bed in
her room and she would go into Harry's small
room where his cramped single bed (he had had
the same one since a child) would more than fit
her shrinking frame . . . innocent old woman . . .
innocent that is of H's abhorrence of ever bringing
anyone else there again . . . and in her senility the
incident had gratefully faded from her mind, while
with Harry it had grown, even assuming monstrous proportions. He had, and dare he even
admit the shadow of this to himself, wished for,
or, rather, would take some vestige of comfort in
the tragedy of her death . . . since she would take
that image to her grave with her. So, as the world
pursued its course around the sun, heading for the
extreme of its revolution . . . as the ice-caps were
melting dangerously fast to the consternation of
Arctic scientists, as the great San Andreas Fault
was shifting and the Russians were completing
their conquest of Mars with the first manned
spacecraft to that planet . . . Harry stood at the
edge of time with the memories of his life
engulfing him like a raging sea with each memory
pulling him this way and that . . . no rest or calm,
so poor they were in joy. His mother prayed and
that eased her tears, and made plans for a fictional
woman . . . his father we cannot here mention . . .
not now, except to say that he carried his portion
of the world and did not pass it to others . . . 'have
I,' he thought, 'have I carried mine' . . . and the
pathetic gesture of wanting so badly to touch
the exhibit's hand at this moment, and his heart

beating for nothing... *since he would do nothing* ... all this would have further reinforced his sense of futility had not a shriek wrenched him away and he was startled to see that the woman and man engaged in fellatio had been disturbed by an irate looking female in a hat who was wielding an umbrella and quite obviously had struck the naked woman's bottom with it since an ugly red weal had already begun to flower. H then turning to the other exhibit saw that they had stopped eating and were watching just like him ... they could be affected after all. On the way back home chewing over the day's adventures on the 172 bus, H was suddenly struck by what the title 'The Circle Line Shall Survive' meant, for him anyway. He may have drawn a coarser meaning than one was meant to elicit but it obviously satisfied H since a smile broke from his face as the bus eased its way into Bethnal Green Road.

From My Point of View

'Of course I like the feeling of a full cunt,' she
thought '... I mean, who doesn't ... and by full I
mean choked full, stuffed full, filled with meat.
And do I question whose meat? Yes, sometimes I
can afford the luxury of discrimination and yes
I do like to be kissed occasionally and not just
wham, bam – put the kettle on love. I do like a
man who's gentle and considerate ... kisses me
tenderly and doesn't just ram his hands up my
skirt to his salvation, being a warm, wet, receptacle
for his seminal deposits. Yet how often, sitting in
my bed-sitting room, do I get a call from someone
I really like, and yet more often as not it's some
Joe I met last year failing in his little black book
(his fuck directory well thumbed) to find his usual
bird clusters at home. Rings me – a vaguely
remembered bird he met at an equally vague,
party or pub ... and what the hell ... 'let's try
this one,' thinks he ... 'Hallo, yes ... who? ... Joe
who? ... Oh!? ... Well ... OK, I'll meet you in
the ...' usually some grotty pub he hangs out
in ... not dinner, Oh no ... 'Thought we'd have a
drink.' He splurges out on two large gins in the
hope of. Should say no really, hell rotten no! ...
But boredom mates uneasily with loneliness pro-
ducing an offspring unbeloved, call desperation,
fuck it ... I brush my teeth to ameliorate my faggy

throat, change my tights and knickers (or maybe just my knickers) put in my cap which I loathe wearing all the time and head out. Thus equipped to face the world at large with my little plastic membrane holding back the anxious creatures that the monster lets loose from his bow ... still, I'm out ... I'm in the air ... I'm using my voice and I see and smell ... I'm paid attention to. I am bought ... all right, so it's only a drink but I am bought it. I live like the rest of my human fraternity ... smile, do I, and act like I too belong to the human race again, instead of sitting on my bed wondering, as I stare at the walls of my prison sanctuary, wondering how I shall endure another bestial night ... tormented by the sounds of music being played in the upstairs rooms and their voices laughing oh so loudly ... what can be so funny to make people laugh that loudly ... I never remember laughing like that ... what special ingredients fill their words and gestures to evoke such joy ... perhaps it seems especially loud to me who am bathed in so much silence ... sometimes I can't sleep (so inconsiderate they) and their laughter always tinkles on into the small hours ... but it's lovely when there is silence again ... then we are the same ... our silence is shared by all ... sitting there dreaming about kitchens with large wooden tables and chairs gathered round, cooking for my man's friends who come and chat idly, while I, pinafored, prepare ... I like that (liberation? ... I don't want liberating, I want imprisoning ... suffocating in the arms of my man) ... I want him to ask me to make special things ... I want him to *be* a bit late from the pub, what the hell, what's a half-hour or even an hour ... you enjoy yourself darling ... No I won't come to the pub I'd rather get the food ready and so I would, he's with me for life why hold back his separate precious hours, and I lay it out beautifully. My mother used to nag my father for tardiness of only ten minutes ... lucky woman didn't know how being alone and waiting for a man, any man, one might have to wait for years ... never mind ten minutes, she didn't know how lucky she was. Poor dad blustering in and chastised until his food wouldn't go down any more ... until the chastisement so consumed him that he vomited out a thrombosis brought about through a heavy surfeit of nag, and then ma *had* him, really and truly had him all to herself ... each day ... every minute was hers ... there he was upstairs, paralysed, in bed and whimpering for his cup of tea ... and wasn't she solicitous then, but of course who has to stay home and work to support us, why I am the inheritor of that raging twisting mouth ... or the deeds thereof since her venom's rewards fall to me ... and who wants a bride of forty when eventually he kicked it, poor dad, and I left home ... hardly a virgin and barely anything ... except ... what could we do then, a girl of twenty and her boyfriend in the hall, standing up since sweet mum would hang around as if twisted for her own loss of male protuberance she therefore wished to share her empty hole with me or share her anguish ... 'don't be too long dear,' she'd whine from the living room ... 'you've got work tomorrow,' as if I didn't have work every day and face the gloomy and drab departments of perpetual boredom and obligation ... the poor guys in the cold hallway kissing me goodnight ... with a sharp frottage against my taffeta (it was then and when it spun around in the dance hall it lifted like petals surrounding a stamen) fed up guys rubbing their hard passion against me in the passage way, while mother is straining her ears from the living room ... and because it was a dark hallway and wretched ma calling, it made urgency for emission that more desperate, whereas a friendly cuddle on the couch and Billy Eckstein on the gramophone would have coaxed a more lasting appreciation ... The hall was furtive, made dark for speed not relaxation, as if what cannot be expressed in warmth and comfort but needs alleys and hall-ways, is something of a more dirty nature ... where the only demands are satisfaction ... so unknowingly but malevolently she condemned my young chances to dirt snatched and mangled ... wet pants and *no* love ... only their shuddering young bodies grabbing me ... their beards still soft ... their hips swivelling blindly against my mount of Venus ... and their poor throbbing hearts emptying their keen and youthful passion amidst sighs not unmixed with guilt for being condemned to alleyways, hallways and the dark recesses of tenements ... 'Let's go up here love,' he cajoles, at the inviting gloom of a staircase in some adjacent building smelling of cats and stale piss ... 'it's OK love, it's dark ... please ... it's all right ... no one can see us ... please ...' Oh ... their young kisses sweeter than wine ... but they seldom came back ... I yielded too easily ... too hurt by my strained home, I wished to compen-sate, for that uncharitable guilt-ridden place by giving them that, which in their young impetuous hearts, they hoped I'd hold on to ... their burning silken pricks were desperate as so often I'd let their juices run onto my hand but their hearts grew rigid as their members softened ... as if my hand in their eyes was scummed for ever. They wanted a picture of something else, a picture of something that should have been more precious to me. They liked coming . . . gasping and quivering in the final sun-burst of their lust but wanted the ache to last and not be assuaged that easily . . . too easily. They pictured too many other bodies being satisfied against this mound of flesh and lavender water (I used it then and sometimes still do) . . . and while the race was theirs that night and peaceful dreams theirs, the hopes of continuance died as if hope needs to be fed slowly for the thing one hopes for to have any real worth. 'One must always struggle for something worthwhile in life,' mother would simper . . . but why should I make them struggle . . . when I don't want them to. Perhaps I should force myself . . . they seldom phoned again and the years drifted by with a succession of young hard bodies and yards and yards of their white stiffened skin bursting in my hands like crushed fruit . . . I became bolder . . . Did I care? No! and for what . . . the plague of parents, and of dad whom I truly did love, invests one at birth with such an awful magnitude of responsibility that one can't say no, and leave them to make do, can't leave home and make the nest needed to live . . . breathe and play Billy Eckstein . . . make coffee and gently dissuade their advances . . . for now anyway . . . win them gradually when trust grows from knowledge and affection and at least we could sit on the sofa and talk . . . I'll cook beautiful dinners . . . such whimpering idle romances drifted down like snow while some brute is fucking me under the staircase . . . stockings torn, knickers around my knees and he's fumbling to get it in deeper but my knees are trapped by my knickers and won't spread . . . he's cursing and pushing and hurting . . . Oh so shameless am I now . . . who cares now? . . . what honour do I have to

protect? ... No! I will not take my knickers off ...
I insist ... shades of black comedy, I have my
point of honour ... On my knickers I make the
last stand of respectability ... my worn shreds of
scruples ... let them fuck me but I won't go out
of my way to take my knickers off and stuff them
in my handbag ... 'What am I, a whore?' ... he
laughs and heaving me up by the ass he affords
himself a good position and I feel his jets
squandering themselves in me and he withdrawing
almost as fast ... no passion was extinguished
quicker than this one. I stand ... weakly in that
black staircase ... my smells mingling with the
odour of dustbins and the vast effluvium that
humanity discharges into them ... so much keener
are the smells now after the act ... and watch him
wiping his prick with a soiled crumpled handkerchief. 'You wanna borrow it love?' ... his voice
held just the faintest note of compassion as if he
too, unburdened of nature's blind demands – of
no matter how, and where, and to whom – empty
it into something! – was able to let float back into
his heart a slender recognition of a person with
whom he had shared an evening, from the first
dance, all smiles and jokes and carefulness to its
ultimate shameful ending.

She went weekly to the same dance hall with the
twisting glass chandelier in the centre, and
whereas a few years ago she was always
accompanied by her friend Doris, Doris having
got engaged and then well and truly pregnant now
made it necessary for her to go alone ... All her
friends got boyfriends one by one and although at
first she wouldn't go alone and went to the pictures instead, she found the dark wombs of the
cinema too unbearable and hated the end when

she'd walk home, made even lonelier by the
romantic and exciting lives of the screen heroes.
One day she decided to go by herself to the Mecca
dance hall and since Mecca is the holy and
religious centre of the world, the salvation for an
entire race, it seemed natural that she would find
solace there . . . on occasion she would bump into
her friends with their fellers and join them at their
table, but always felt slightly oppressed by their
little knowing glances which she'd exaggerate into
hideous thoughts of 'what's the slag doing by
herself' . . . and she would gradually recline to the
outer perimeter of the dance floor . . . in the shade
so to speak and be dragged out to dance by one
lonely man after another who first would eye her
suspiciously and nervously. How a woman alone
is a stigma . . . and yet attractive . . . dangerous,
why alone? They think . . . something in her casts
her out from the norm . . . the giggling girls . . .
the confident groups . . . something that makes her
slightly unwholesome, as if diseased . . . yet offers
up sweet, sickly goods if you want to take the
risk . . . still the element of danger . . . makes her
sought after by the kind of men whom the robust
directness of youth would wilt . . . who would not
risk the light-hearted rebuff of young girls sure of
their attractiveness who are waiting for strong, just
as direct, young men . . . but the lone figure in
taffeta, now that is for me, man thinks, poses no
threat . . . only the remote element of a more nagging threat; no outward risk of humiliation . . .
possibly though the inward one, working on the
vitals of the body of the brain . . . She moaned
inside herself . . . 'how unnatural that I am a leper
just because my mother had a raging mouth' . . .
the two things were somehow now inseparable, as
if her mother had really cursed a twisted fate on

her that she could not untangle ... so rather than try and change this situation she would make her mother eat her satisfaction. 'I like it here,' she mused ... Through the years she had watched the faces grow up from tender, young, energetic and pretty things to smart (still young), mascaraed ladies, teasing and jiving with their beaux and it gave her not the slightest taste of jealousy or remorse ... she was glad that she felt no bitterness but was able to enjoy the gaiety, even if the young and pretty things eyed her suspiciously as she, strange, caked make-up, wallflower smelling too violently of lavender water, waited. One night early in the spring there was a warm snap in the air ... it was the first time she could go out without the heavy top-coat and thus be spared the awful queue after the dance when she would have to stand with all the chattering excited girls giggling about who was taking them home and exchanging notes ... If she hadn't found anyone to take her home, she as often as not would persist right to the end of the evening when most people had been paired off. She would nervously await the remnants of mankind, the lonely and the plain, or the just plain psychotic who, also unlucky, would desperately eye the last possibilities and odd tired wrecks to sort some salvage from the human female shapes that littered the outer ring. They, poor single women would feel even more vulnerable at this stage and creep nearer each other as if they too had friends, or ask each other for lights, pass nervous small smiles at each other, but still keep alert, since to pass out of the Mecca with a gentleman hooked to your arm was still something worth waiting for. ... not to go alone and leave alone ... Show them – the young, the proud, the pretty – that I too can claim some happiness. So

feeling spared of the queue and in the optimism
that spring brings, she was determined that night
not to wait until the end and if nothing suitable
came along, damn it – she'd go home. She went
to the box-office clutching her money and set it
down 'one please', but this time did she sense
something as one man in an ill-fitting tuxedo
leaned over the ear of the cashier, sense something
like a cold blast? She did. For the lady in the box-
office said ... 'I'm so sorry dear but I'm afraid
you're barred' ... The queue of people behind
her stopped their eager chattering, except for one
joker, innocently unaware of the respect that
one must pay in the face of tragedy, who sang 'Oh
why are we waiting' to the tune of 'Oh Come All
Ye Faithful'. ... 'So sorry,' the lady repeated ...
'What have I done,' she thought, 'what have I
done except act as a host to all those multitudes,
to ease their agony ... like a comfort station you
might say, *something you need when you're
desperate* ...' She stood there as if the world had
jolted to a halt and there could be no place you
could possibly go since one's home was now a ruin
of unmatchable stones ... she couldn't speak ...
stood there as if it hadn't happened as if the cashier would witness the terrible effect which needed
no words and would be humbled by the naked
show of human agony and permit her to enter
what now indeed seemed like a Mecca. She didn't,
she just looked ... and eventually said, 'Would
you like to see the manager?' but then as if
annoyed by the inordinate amount of time this
trivial incident was taking, the man in the box-
office, who usually doubled as a bouncer, nipped
nimbly out and took her to one side to let in
the queue that had grown considerably. They all
glanced at her half curious, half hostile ... what's

the slut done now? scrawled across their eyes ...
the man in the tuxedo spoke quietly, 'We don't
want any trouble but you're barred, ducky ... all
right ... know what I mean ... nothing personal
like' ... thought she, 'What do they suspect me
of? What do they suspect could be my reasons
over all these years for coming here ...
"Commerce" ... is that what's in their filthy
minds?' ... she said nothing ... she had become
in minutes flint from velvet ... He continued but
sensed a pain in her he hadn't expected ...
especially from a scrubber ... 'Give the place a
bad name, on the game you know ... get rid of
it.' Higher orders had thus embellished his mind
with such commands that he uncomfortably
obeyed. 'You know,' he added sympathetically,
'there's a club down the road called "The Carou-
sel", you'll be OK there.' He made the suggestion
based on the assumption that what he had heard
was true and therefore his advice was charitable
and not vicious. She knew the place it was and
read only venom in his words and from that
instant began to hate the male part of the human
race. She walked away from the Mecca with its
twisting globe and ladies' invitation waltzes, with
the familiar sound that same band always had,
from the familiar smell and initial excitement
when you first enter that huge cavern wherein
may lie your future ... she walked away from
it ... for ever ... She stayed home for a year until
poor dad, perhaps willingly, seeing his treasured
forty-year-old daughter's plight, gave up the ghost
in one almighty shriek of joy.

She left home, determined to find that love-laced
sanctuary with a nice kitchen and sofa and saved
for a record player. For now, rents being high –

she lived in a bedsitter and found that loneliness just doesn't suddenly disappear . . . when you have lived with it for so long it emanates from your entire being . . . when introduced, even, you are afraid that the stranger will sense it on you, as if some disagreeable odour lingers that cannot be washed out. Sometimes, though rarely, she was hauled away when her local closed for an after-hours drinks party, more to make up the number than any cognisance of her being . . . let alone her name . . . but still she was free . . . 'aren't I,' she thought.

Perhaps the caller on the telephone this evening is nice . . . I remember speaking to someone who was quite nice about a year ago at the office party . . . perhaps it's him . . . she sprayed some lavender water on her arms and not too carefully put lipstick on . . . 'hell, what can a girl do at ten pm when she's been sitting in drinking a few gins?' . . . At a pub in Kentish Town a guy named Harry was standing at the bar . . . waiting.

Going Down

Coming up to surface with a mouthful of blood ...
cheeks reddened, with a thick gore glistening ...
looking for all the world like an impish school-
boy's ravishing of a jar of strawberry jam, was not
Harold's idea of a perfect evening. Certainly he
felt no qualms in going down on her, since he truly
loved sucking ... it drew him that much closer to
the object of his need ... to knowing a woman
with his shameless intimacy, to bring the inner
sanctity of his mouth to her groin ... how fussy
one is, so particular what one puts in one's
mouth ... nose quivering at yesterday's milk ...
yet the heat of desire sacrificed any cautious fore-
thought in Harold's mind as he sneaked like a
moon probe across the white valleys of his lover,
whispering small licklacks over hills ... nosing
towards the musky heavy odour of Sybil's cunt
whereupon his head voyaging south to her feet
would stop, his forearm prising open her thighs ...
detecting the slight coppery or metallic taste which
he didn't find too pleasant, flanks spread apart
like opening a giant fleshy flower ... or she'd pour
her buttocks onto his hands whilst Harold's
tongue worked like an erratic snake ... up and
down ... pressing, chewing ... breathing through
his mouth as he licked and sensed her warm
odours entering his throat ... his cheeks were

chafed sometimes, as if she secreted some corrosive acid (could he have licked up the residue of urine?) ... did it matter down there dark, thigh strangled, hot, barely breathing ... imagining in that florid hot-house the endless parade of his fantasies ... moments in the underground, thick summer days ... the sliding doors are open, a passing train in the other direction ... its motion sends a little gust of wind into the carriage ... invisible fingers delicately lift the thin cotton dresses, revealing all too briefly (rapid hands flutter, tug, cover) the gates of nirvana, Valhalla, heavy in all colours, a riotous symphonic concerto of crutch ... 'No, not one's earnest, coarse fingers in those greasy sockets *but* my mouth between those marble thighs' ... such thoughts were the armoury of his endeavour, fuelling him to enable sucking Sybil's rather smelly cunt. He could be stoking the drain, blocked up in the garden, she stank so bad at times. So his habit of breathing through his mouth – more odourless that way – was safer ... other times she smelt as fresh as new bread and earnestly swore how twice daily she'd wash her hole, even so ... perhaps it was something she ate. She had soft pubic hairs, that was all right by Harold ... he could no more suck the inside of a cunt whose garden had coarse (brillo-pad) hair, than lick assholes (reserved for beauties of extraordinary loveliness); shit and beauty in Harold's mind never co-existed, or at least obviously as in a farty old slag ... the thicker the hair, the stronger the smell, Harold fancied ... even if not scientifically true, the feeling of it made it true, so sucking hairy mediterranean cunts, those hairy-legged Greeks and Italians, was *verboten* ... he would retch at the idea, whilst black cunt though legendarily famed for magic properties was unimaginable horror ... the downy hair of celts-saxons-nordics was fine and soft ... Sybil was fair, reasonably attractive with good teeth and blue eyes – except the occasional rupture of acne on her back made Harold feel desolate ... sometimes in bed, he'd be alarmed to see the shining yellow beads of those eruptions and drive down fast, suck and forget ... would remember only the mouths about to speak, the impeccable panties, the frozen eyes, stern yet yielding as sirens, forbidding your mind to interpret the mystery of the picture the gentle wind exposed ... seeing these faces he could endure sucking at Sybil's greasy and sometimes smelly exit, while she would aid with her spit greased hand on his cock – her index finger one inch up his anus (concession in recent months) – but sucking, God forbid ... no ... she couldn't ... 'try – just once' ... 'OH NO I'D BE SICK!' 'Just a little lick then.' 'Please Harold, don't make me, give me time, I will when I'm used to you' ... so he gave her time ... for a year he had been travelling down to that brown cleft, opening to shades of pink ... and flaps and slivers opening like torn meat in the butchers, it was an animal, mysteriously armed with feelers, or those monstrously swollen jelly fish floating in the Aegean ... sometimes he could take the daylight suck ... other times he could not bear to see it and took solace deep under the blankets and after he would surface looking like some insane deep-sea diver, a mad drunk feasting on meths, or a predator fresh from the killing of some soft thing ... 'SORRY DARLING, OH MY GOD WASH YOUR FACE! I HAVE JUST COME ON. MY PERIOD! OH SHIT ... HAROLD I'M SORRY, WASH IT' ... Harold's face surfacing like a monstrous shark with bloody mouth dis-

turbed Sybil since she didn't want Harold to see
it ... 'stay there, I'll bring a flannel!' ... but
Harold sensing something odd even down
below ... more bitter than before, acrid even, that
harsh taste ... he didn't stay, was already out of
bed and even rushing to the bathroom aware
of the red spore his fingers left on the wall as he
hastily switched on the light ... 'Oh my God,'
he spat as he spoke ... 'phphaaaaa!' Tried to wash
out his throat under the tap *dare not* look, fuck
no, look in the mirror! But on habit did and
looked like he had been punched hard in the
mouth ... calmly now he took the flannel and
washed carefully every part of his mouth ... kept
washing ... her words broke into the sound of the
busy tap barely audible, scent of fear rising
through them 'OK Harold? ... sorry love ...' So
all these months he had performed his lingual
duties to some indifferent smells and responses ...
had even once smelled shit down there (what *had*
she been up to) ... and the lady, too elegant to as
much as put it in her mouth for five seconds without being ill ... menstruates in my holy mouth ...
fucking menstruates ...

S. I'm regular ... I don't understand.

H. Was it early ... you think so ... a few
days?

S. It must have been ... (*diary hastily
consulted*). Oh dear I forgot the day!
Don't look like that Harry.

H. You are a turd.

S. Harold I'm sorry ... Harold? ... No
don't ... don't, you're mad!

H. (*clasps a large bread-knife while he
shoves his cock in her face*). Put it in your
mouth ... go on pig ... open.

S. Yes Harry, but don't . . . please.

H. Just fucking open your mouth (*holds knife near her throat*) and hold my prick near the balls.

S. Yes Harry . . . Harr . . . mmmn OK.

H. Faster now you pig and squeeze my balls at the same time.

S. (*choking*). mmmmm! . . . chchch! . . . NOOOO! (*withdraws mouth*).

H. I'll kill you Sybil, so help me . . . SUCK IT!

S. OOOh Harry . . . don . . . mmmmn . . .

She hadn't a bad mouth and once she started seemed to go at it with an eagerness which wasn't purely the result of Harry with his pink scrubbed face kneeling over her with a bread knife but bore more the effect of one who, in having no choice, decides the lesser of the two evils is to go ahead and enjoy it. He came . . . screaming . . . and she didn't flinch but licked every drop down . . . licked it clean . . . was it retribution for her accident, or was there something indefinable and unspoken in her which begged the threat of supreme violence in order to unlock what she desperately wanted to give (dare not admit her tastes), longed always to have taken . . . as she lay calmly beside his sleeping body . . . his face broken by waves of peace she felt no more fear and even thought with gratification of her curse . . . his poor bloody mouth . . . she could not restrain a thin smile escaping from the corner of her lips . . . naturally, Harold didn't see it.

The Secret of Capitalism

I have a room . . . that is most important . . . I have a room in an old house but the house is mine. So I have tenants . . . so far so good. I have a nationality and speech. All the things that bring me together as one being are in and outside me. I have a house and a woman in the house . . . that's as it should be . . . I mean, a man should have a woman and have a house to deposit her in so as to have her adjacent to him and vice-versa. She also has a room and visits his room – so she has autonomy which is also most important. They can look out of separate windows onto the streets – which brings me to my street – so I have an address and I receive letters. Without an address nobody will write you a letter . . . so an address increases the possibility of written communication, also a postman will visit you and occasionally ask you to sign a book for special letters. Your house is recorded in the town hall and is part of history, which you as occupier will help to make . . . the house will always be there, perhaps for ever. It is in the deeds of the house and recorded in ancient maps and scrolls and charted for sewage and water flow. All the mysteries of the tides that come to and flow away from the house, nationality, lodgers, own room, language and postal possibilities. Also I have inside and outside two cats . . . both are

tortoiseshell but they are not related ... one of
the cats has one ear which lends her a distinctive
air, and both of these cats play in the garden –
which is also mine ... so now you may see how a
human being is put together gradually to form
a composite entity. Having a house you will also
possess everything within the house and necessary
to the house's comfort but since these things can
be bought as effects they are not worth mention-
ing except in so far as they may throw some light
on you. So far nothing here is mentioned except
the house that is actually bought since you cannot
buy the street or the postman or letters from a
friend, or a woman ... not in this particular
case ... so these things are of a more related
nature by the act of getting a house ... to possess
it, I have a mortgage which is an ancient docu-
ment, not my mortgage but mortgages as such
date back in origin over a thousand years. I have
also a bank in which I deposit or from which I
withdraw money ... therefore like the rest of this
society I have a bank manager. I have an agent
for work as an actor who for some reason never
gets me any work, so I have a bad agent. Also I
have an administrator and part-time secretary who
has an office on the top floor of an old building
which is seedy although her office is a model of
order ... she has an inside toilet which she needs
a key to unlock and then locks up again, although
there is nothing to steal except turds. I have an
accountant, a lawyer and a dentist plus an Arts
Council bursary. I have plays, stories and many
photographs ... the photographs are of a holiday
in Greece and one old one of my sister and
myself in Brighton sitting on the wall of the Black
Rock Swimming Pool, I was ten years old at the
time. I have a literary agent (I forgot to mention

her) ... yes, she is a woman and she too has a secretary and so indirectly they are put to my use, therefore you could say that I have two secretaries, a further one who also works part-time for me, even a small part of the time, and everything or anything that influences her: i.e. her mother feeding her, her boyfriend kissing her or abusing her too: all this serves to affect the five minutes or so every day that she devotes to me in answering the phone or writing letters on my behalf. So, her boyfriend and her mother and father all serve me in some infinitely small but ineluctable part of the complex tapestry which is my life. And whom do I serve? I serve all of them to a degree in that I provide them with a marginal sense of purpose. I serve whom I work with and I serve the audience but they in effect also serve me and partially belong to me ... since it takes a hundred or more to serve me at one sitting but it takes only one of me to serve them but to serve them I am helped by able-bodied people who also serve me as I serve them. The mute point of who serves whom depends on a particular form of philosophic thought which may be elliptical. It also depends on who thinks it first. If the person who is serving me thinks that he is being served by me, before I can state that I am being served by him, then psychologically he may be at an advantage, purely in the thinking of it ... first. Sometimes 200 people will come to see me in a play or see my play ... to reach the theatre they will occupy 200 spaces in buses, cars and taxis and this puts out another 200 who were wanting those particular services and so on with ever-diminishing effects ... So, one can say that the 200 have washed, eaten, planned, telephoned each other and affected throughout this activity a further 1000 people (switchboards, restaurants, cars, parking-space attendants), communicated, read newspaper reports, met each other and eventually walked up the stairs of the building, were anticipatory, sat down and watched the play. At the end of the play, 200 people got up and left the building and in their consequent actions disturbed or affected another 1000 people. In slightly poetic terms they resembled a small tide of humanity seeping into a particular crevice in the rocks and then being pulled out again to dissolve into and swell the greater mass, making no impression on the mass and yet essential to it. The rocks are again revealed much like the seats in the theatre when everyone has gone, except that the inflowing tide has washed clean the rocks whereas in the theatre a charlady goes round in the morning cleaning up. The only cleansing effect might be the purging of unclean spirits and the dissolving of agony through identification. These are side effects and bear no relation to the greater theme of possession. These people go home carrying within them the germ of my play as by contamination and the words and actions of the production flit around inside their minds which may continue for days or even for years, and may even effect the way they move or think about certain subjects ... consequently these people may be serving you indefinitely if not consciously. Of the 200 who come each night, some will die this year and others next year. Since there are approximately 1000 per week in a good week, it would be true to say that some may be dying during the play. The condition of the audience will vary, unrelated to what they are seeing since they brought their own mood with them from sadness to a state of pleasure, others will be in a state of jealousy and others will be made envious by what they imagine is a nice way to earn a living since they are relieved of the boring drudgery of putting a play together and dealing with the temperament of actresses. Some women in the audience will be in the time of their period and wearing appropriate safeguards ... when they talk afterwards in the bar, loudly and pontifically, an X-ray through them would reveal tights, corsets, Tampax, soiled underwear. If one could see through their clothes they would not seem so affected, in fact they would appear silly. Animals never appear silly since they do not wear Tampax or tights. And how ridiculous a dog would look with a cigarette sticking out of his mouth. And yet a human looks more ridiculous. But humans are convinced they look all right because everyone looks stupid in one way or another. During the week the 200 people will talk to another 1000 people, assuming that they mention it to at least five people each during that week which is quite likely. So 1200 people will be affected by each performance to a greater or lesser degree, like a tiny drop of water receding over a limpet as the tide claims it back. So during the entire week, 7200 people including taxi drivers and the milliard diverging pressures will be brought to a streaming confluence by one person moving with a steady pace to his goal. I will be in part responsible for this effect by being a small pool or crevice which will trap a certain part of humanity. They will serve me by washing over me and (metaphorically) leaving behind some of their treasure for the experience. When they buy a ticket they will have contributed, if middle class, one hour, after taxes have been paid, of their labour. So they have contributed not only one and a half hours of concentration plus one hour to travel to the theatre and buy their tickets, but at least another hour in labour, and it will take them after they retrieve their coats, another hour to go home and so all told one has a gain of four and a half hours from each person. That's if one could find a way to use those hours. Of the 200 in the audience each night, 130 would have had bowel motion that day and fifteen would have had sexual intercourse; two would have had sex before coming to the theatre and approximately seventeen will have sex after ... indirectly affected by what they have seen ... I will, in a sense, be in the way of their sex, I will affect the quality of their movements, especially if they were soothed or gratified by what they saw or sensuously aroused. I may therefore increase their satisfaction or curb it. They will talk at length about the play, or briefly. On the other hand they may quarrel violently with each other as to the meaning of the piece since it is open to interpretation and, through this conflict, the man will see he has nothing in common with the woman and decide that night to leave her since this particular play stimulated them both to a statement of intent and measure of their own observations and sensitivity. On the other hand he may, if inflamed, decide to kill her since this is the last straw and he is aghast at how stupid she is and is excited by an overcharge of adrenalin. If he does this I will have a murder on my conscience to a slight degree, diminishing in return to the extent of his own psychosis. This audience comes from separate parts of London and the world and are all brought together by a common interest to one particular building. They will share an experience as one mass no longer part of an anonymous tide but a related one. They will laugh at appropriate lines and hear and smell each other. At the end they will put their hands together in appreciation and this same mass of people will never ever meet again although they were a party to a particular experience and brought together by chance. They will never exploit this strange fact. You may think that the same thing applies to someone on a bus and that the group of people on that particular bus are congregated together by the same laws of chance and likewise could exploit that. However, that is not quite a fair analogy since to choose that particular play suggests a wealth of undercurrents, taste and inclinations, curiosity and desire particular to the 200 who chose to see that play out of 10 million people. The critics come on the first night and write about you. Their reviews are read carefully or glanced at, picked through, raced through, mostly ignored, read anxiously, audaciously, arrogantly, sadly or happily, even cynically by 1 million people in five or six papers. 3 million times will your name be printed in offset litho and the next day someone else's new play will crush your name and work into limbo but not quite ... for a few moments that day you shake hands with the King; for those few seconds that you are there under his gaze (he representing the nation) you hold history in your hand, the last line of 1000 years of kings ... and so you hold onto that moment. If one froze that moment you would be there for ever, and time having a subtle way of stopping now and again gives that impression. How does that audience know that it will ever leave the theatre. As far as they are concerned, they are there for ever. It is only in their knowledge that it must end. But one can never be really sure, especially since one is deprived of certain sensory measuring stimuli such as daylight deepening into night or changes of temperature.

In the theatre there is no time that can be measured since one is bathed in a constant light and the steady drone of words and sounds may never end, but it does and in that way lies sanity: only in the sure knowledge that it will. In the same way the critics' columns focus the nation's attention on you 3 or 4 million times over and if a certain paper reviewed it, no matter what copy of it you picked up it will be there, it will not subtly change ... but later, for instance the following morning, people in the poorer areas are wiping their asses and wrapping their chips in your hopes for immortality. Others are throwing it on the litter heap of yesteryear's editions where the corpses of old news welcome you on the heap waiting to be used for other purposes. You may find yourself in the toilets that serve parks and public places. The newspapers are torn up into squares ... and on one of the squares there you are, or one-millionth of you is finding yourself wiping clean the excessive excrement on some stranger's ass. But, as she or he craps, they may have taken into their hands the strips of paper in readiness and, glancing down with the idle curiosity that people have in toilets, have examined the bit of news before reaching their final apotheosis and then glueing your legend to their sphincter. As they read it, during which time they have laid well tunnelled and twisted lavas of molten shit, they are seized by a sudden notion (time and place being conducive to deep thinking) to see this particular play. 'Hmmmmmm' ... they murmur ... 'How interesting' ... Crappppbbrasperyyythpp ...! This is possible ... but to get back to other things besides the critics who serve me with their reviews ... I do have other things; for instance, I have ulcers. I have to drink milk when they start

74

inflaming me, when a little worrisome fire is ignited in my belly in the upper part ... I have a fridge for the milk in which I also keep the cat food. I can still remember when we didn't have fridges years ago in the suburbs and had instead a cupboard with mesh netting ... this is about the time when I had that photo taken with my sister in Brighton. Everything went off quite quickly and the milk was kept under running water in the basin to keep cool. I have had my fridge for eight years and my mother gave it to me, who had it for ten years before that ... so it is a sturdy fridge, you might say. I do have a friend or two ... probably two reasonably good friends and several acquaintances and two lots of neighbours ... my friends, if I include all the people that I know reasonably though not well, would be about fifty ... and I know perhaps ten of those intimately, if not lovingly. Each of these fifty whom I know reasonably well, perhaps knows another fifty people reasonably, so I will have a possible cache of 2500 people who may be aware of me reasonably, and these 2500 may know another fifty which would bring me only twice removed the possibility of knowing or the knowledge of 125,000 people, which is a lot ... so, I am surrounded by my house, my fridge, room, woman, spare room, windows, literary agent, photographs and, oh yes, I forgot my books. These 200 books bring to me the accumulated knowledge of 200 people who acquired this knowledge throughout their lives and the experience of other books plus teachers and families of, say, 100 per writer, which brings me the distilled experience of 20,000 people all together ... all in my one room. The million who have read me in the columns (I now begin stocktaking), the thousands who have seen me on the stage and the dozens whose sexual experience I have unconsciously affected, my two cats, my accountant, lawyer, part-time secretary, two neighbours and a garden, my ulcers and the memories of an old cupboard, a street which is part of history and an address, the possible knowledge of 125,000 people which is a lot and the possibility of stopping time. Plus the woman upstairs ... surrounded as I say by these points of reference which eventually must run into millions ... I wonder why I am often lonely and desolate.

Pictures

At approximately ten strokes a second, he calcu-
lated, 600 to a minute and aided by olive oil,
Brylcreem or vegetable oil – the best lubricator
but with a tendency to the finest insulation – at
600 strokes a minute, three minutes would
produce 1800 strokes, then there would be the
thankful emission from his grateful prick . . . his
eyes fixed at the usual spot on the ceiling and
made a tight link to that crack or hair which
seemed to be painted in (loose hair from decor-
ator's brush?), and across this link, like an electric
beam, travelled a lexicon of images, so inventive
was the mind in this state, the translation of this
source of inspiration to a painter's hand would
have filled the National Gallery . . . a thousand
variations of Judith's thighs, the spread open red
mouth of her womb flashed on and off the ceiling
like a crazy stroboscope, the pictures twisted and
dissolved into swollen vulvas, deep dark shadows
opening up to snow, glistening misty forests and
tropical dank flowers unpeeling . . . the cock
strained at this point to brace itself, a snake about
to spit, but flagged again from over-exposure,
these particular movies had seen too many re-
releases . . . new scenes flashed on dredged up
from the ancient vaults of his mind, some would
tend to get confused like an actor in repertory

mixing up his parts, or he'd jump-cut from scene to scene (incredible editor) hold one for a few seconds longer, or freeze a frame, slow dissolve, leap from mouth to mouth and cunt to cock in three or two shots, old fading experiences mixed with fiction ... hot greedy mouths, men's, from infantile experiences, and pubescent painful experiences which changed into unsuccessful affairs, then fictionalised into brilliant seductions; lone female fingers prised out his cock and lovingly swallowed it ... but the images based on fiction did not have the staying power that truth etched into the mind, and faded only too quickly leaving that same crack of hair on the ceiling ... and the silence ... broken only by the soft susurus; the whipping flesh and quickening breath, and the lone solo instrumentalist in the room, empty usually, except for a prostrate outstretched body tapping out the relentless morse-code on his cock ... does any one pick up the signals? Lonely, dedicated wanker of the endless nights, surrounded by the riotous horny guests of his imagination ... again the men's mouths; experience of darkened cinemas, cheap flea-pits in the remote suburbs, running *Spring in Park Lane* to the memory of humiliation and fear of getting caught, furtive eyes, sticky handkerchiefs, smelly Turkish baths; these had, between moments of electric stimulation, also a vaguely deadening effect. The whore who watched him spill his seed into her discarded knickers was good ... he was primed to come on that but no, it would leave him with a bad memory at the end ... so he switched it off and flashed Judith back on (her greasy black knickers held the stage for a further 200/300 strokes) and then he projected a whole series of flashbacks with the speed of a remote-control slide projector ... swelling vast cock exposed to the hungry eyes of Scottish teacher (incredible grip she had), emptying vast quantities of spunk into the endless open mouths of women like the beaks of hungry birds ... on and on, fiction smearing onto fact, male converging into female ... the cock, proud strutting creature, was tiring of the years of service of penal solitude within the shackles of this man's fist, wearying of the endless roles ... was it this man's joy, his solitary guard against the vivid constraint of truth, the EMPTI-NESS, MUST IT BE A WALL OF FLESH AROUND IT AND HOW LONG CAN IT BE SO, THE WEARYING FLESH? ... Soon it will be over ... but to end on a good one ... it was straining to spurt ... to send the owner back to the limbo from whence he came, and the flesh back to the comparative sanctuary of darkness and peace ... the rhythm slows down ... not so fast, hold it back, wh*oa* boy not so fast! Hold it back ... do not spill the precious lotion in vain on the memory of some old slut ... hold fast the gates until the cunt computer makes the right selection for a hit ... a whisper 'more oil' ... the needle of his desire scanning back and forth every possible combination of pictures ... yes ... the girl in the tube ... her crossing legs accidentally exposing to his snaking eyes the instant explosion of her tri-angle (moon-white – sanctified by Diana white), she repeated this action which made him squirm for the rest of the journey, hands in his pockets he mutilated his flesh and during this time she did not refuse him the sight that was his altar on that voyage through the black tunnels of the city ... she left the train delicately, uncrossed her thighs more overtly; do you see the contours, her thighs soft white tender dreamy ... she's gone ... the

ensuing adventure of what might have happened
had he had the courage to follow made many an
interesting story and often provided the perfect
climax to his jerkings ... he would start at the
same point and go over it carefully, second by
second ... the colour of hair, smile, the shape of
leg, shade of underwear ... it was beautiful; just
once or twice before reaching his conclusion he'd
interject with Judith to test the strength of his
present story, and satisfied that Judith was endow-
ing the performance with far less fuel, continued
the fantasy in the train, the smile ... the legs ...
faster, the colour of knickers ... faster ... mix
now with spit (mortar and pestle) up to normal
speed ... 600 a minute, even faster ... 700 ...
750 ... the picture on the ceiling increasing to
intensity ... her open joints, his fingers engaged
in thick warm flesh discovering the new
continent ... her panties were a holy veil across
his face ... HIS cock became quite still, breathless,
waiting for the explosion. The INEVITABILITY
OF IT ... HIS flesh was blushing like a throttled
colonel (he was in love with her desperately) ...
a thick pearl formed in the smile of his knob
like a tear ... (desperately loved) (POURING)
he licked ... (SPURTING IN TWO RISING
JETS) ... her ... pumping out the last spasm in a
thin web still reaching high ... smelled her (first
strangling the last juices of his cock's throat) ...
loved her always ... the picture faded abruptly ...
leaving the crack with the hair ... he wiped the
cooling spunk off his belly with four or five sheets
of Kleenex ... you could depend on the girl in the
train.

She or a Day in Brighton

As she ran for the bus her hair would jump and
impersonate a waterfall spilling over a cataract.
The sun almost heaved itself out of the sky this
morning like a difficult birth ... it poured from
torn wounds yellow tears into the sea. Suddenly,
before the contraction of a pupil exposed to sun
from woolly cloud, the sea transformed itself into
a lake of emeralds and then a cold palace of
verdigris ... marmoreal ... then purpureal. White
flecks are spat up as invisible demons blow
down ... white flecks as the blue paint which is
chipped away, exposes the underneath ... from
the sea Clytemnestra gathers squids whose special
ink dyes the silks that Agamemnon will tread on
his triumphant return from Troy ... she will
plunge her dagger into the same silk, wrapping
him in it as he steps from his bath ... The sea
smells sharp today, tangy, fishy, ozone laced ...
its smells filter through the curtains and linger on
the walls, its invisible antennae crawl through the
bricks and under the window panes ... slide across
her pillow over several thousand fine golden
spears that sprout from her skull ... they lay like
a field of corn ... golden and still ... so her hair
lay like flax ready to be woven ... and the smell
of the sea crawled over the pillow and into her
head, up her nostrils and floated over the special

nerve colonies of her brain begging for recognition . . . and the gentle susurus as claws of wet green tickled small shingle, tinkling, whispering, found the curvature of her ear, spinning round the tunnels of flesh and beating tiny taps or small filibrations on her drums . . . the two effects (smell and sound) were conjoined as if by plot . . . those waves would also serve to prise open the memories that will seep out gradually and hover in the Sunday morning breakfast air smelling of tea, bacon, toast, polish and dead things . . . like the memory of old loves and loving, perpetuated after the corpse of a kipper has been devoured and is fleshily stimulating the devourer . . . the tray is left quietly outside the door . . . the tea and marmalade make a small fire glowing inside the packages of skin that swell and yield . . . those presents to one's partner in the early morning blue with white buttery tinged clouds peering through the window . . . her Edwardian nightie lay on the bed like a promise of eventual fulfilment . . . after we arose it was lain across the bed by the chambermaid as though a live thing was still in it . . . it was silk and the touch of it gave pleasure to the maid who would hold it in both hands and on opening them, let the nightie pour from her hands like it was a living thing . . . like a cat was pouring out of her hands.

Stardom

The gases in the universe are floating and spinning away at the speed of light, away from us, everything expands. The spirals of millions of stars are an emission from the collision of invisible gases gripping, passing through each other, exploding a chain of circumstances that will be repeated microcosmically. Carbon and Helium fuse, rolling over and over, and detonates one thousand million stars. In one man's emission from a full penis will be a thousand million spermatozoa ... these sperms took forty-five days to reach maturity ... out of all of them only one valiant strong-tailed beast will survive, only one will in its travels along those dark river beds of blood and orgasmic secretions find a world to penetrate, from a journey through the warm labyrinths of inner space the equivalent of millions of miles. Blindly its will, such as it must have, and desire to be, guides it to penetrate the celestial orb which comes floating down to meet it, they greet with little formality and lock in an embrace that will not cease. Not anyway until one has wrested the secret from the other. Thus an emission of sperm resembles a galaxy, in a silken glittering silvery web of froth; floating in space, it would spiral like the milky way or like cream in coffee, or paint in oil, or ink dropped into water ... The gases create the emission by confrontation and osmosis, some mad god is populating the universe with the wild excesses of his passion, if there are ten thousand million stars in our galaxy, the Milky Way, our own village, and one thousand Milky Ways, soon where will we find room to move? Will not space be obliterated through overpopulation? However the interstellar galactic social heads will control space over-pack by a series of thermonuclear suns that will go spinning into new orbits obliterating as they go. Errant asteroids will be armed and sent on new paths pulled out of their normal gravitational orbits and collide with living world centres.

At that particular time I may be just at the point of spraying my burning vaporous seed into the womb of an earthly flesh garden to grow more cherubic plants of plasma/bone/thought, when the end will happen, my own universe be disintegrated and plans of future galaxies destroyed at source. My body, stained with all her viscous stigmata, my emptying vessels screeching from hot pipes, the creatures spitting, racing, hurtling through the black hole (a giant succuum, or sucking vacuum), my teeth breaking themselves on raw bone in the absurd excesses of passion and my fingers brilliantly ringed in tunnels of flesh-warm. At that moment, the moment when my spine receives the benediction of a fugue played by her delicate fluttering fingers, will she, dark, tight pupils, accept the vision through the window of a giant sun scorching through the night like a vast lion about to devour us? Fires already raging everywhere and still one million miles away, travelling at two-sixteenths the speed of light, the decision will have to be swiftly made of how we wish to spend our last five earthly minutes or climb into the

time-machine and hurtle off to a more clement
century.

Eventually we were too deeply locked into each
other's system to disentangle, without subsequent
emotional damage, she held fast to my hips until
she came ... screaming, and I too followed, and
just then the fire was upon us and sucked the air
out of our lungs before crushing the planet into a
charred heap leaving a black hole ... We were
just in time.

The Assless Dictator or Homage to Miss Gascoigne

The sea joined sky, married . . . flowed into each
other, mixed . . . fertilised, new colours . . . became
an inseparable sheet . . . of slate, jade, and deli-
quescent marble veined with cracks and splits of
white . . . the mists moved over the water . . .
glazing and caressing, rolled over the waves, rolled
over the clawed creatures scuttling . . . August 4th
is a day of peace . . . I sit outside the hotel in a
wicker chair . . . the receptionist wears a thin, fine
Victorian blouse over a gossamer thin bra or
halter that can only weigh an ounce . . . her breasts
are heavy but not too much, more a gentle
heaviness . . . almost plangent, soft weight, warm
crushables, squeezable, sway very delicately . . .
the nipples dark, just barely perceived by the scanning eye that crawls over the body like a green
leech . . . the sea now divides itself from the sky
as if it had dripped out of heaven and now floats
heavily . . . the division while clear is not yet sharp
but a soft bleeding in of colours . . . the edge of
blotting paper . . . the sea is heavy and the small
waves curl over each other like small kittens
rolling and playing and showing flecks of white
paws . . . the atmosphere smells clean and fishy,

seaweed salt and spray, but is cool and damp, and while the sun beats down heavily and invisibly the clouds spread out to prevent us having any of it ... yet thin small tracks of yellow almost seem to seep through but become scattered ... soft-bodied sea anemones flop and squirm in the glaucous green for them, for smears of sudden warmth. In her pants rests an immutable secret, subject to the same forces as the sea ... her underskin softly holds an active small beast ... this beast has a maw which gently holds your future and your present might ... and is the entrance to an embryonic cave as surely as is the sea ... the sea spills out life from its crucible fertilised by the sun's shafts that break themselves into the green ... the sea wears away at the cliffs ... the cliffs, friable and stiff, crumble over the years ... they crumble like a giant edifice topples in slow motion, it crumbles and is sucked into the sea whose thin rasping claws gather it up ... small shelled creatures make homes there and dart in and out with delicate antennae the colour of coral ... her caves tempt you crazily to hold discourse with her eyes ... the first orbits of the journey to unknown spaces in her vast and fertile universe of untold delights ... her eyes are brown and moving, within which galaxies, harbouring many different systems, can be seen evolving ... the sea's horizon remains in her eyes ... the tides float across them ... when the tide comes in I will enter and be carried in her body's liquids to her inner depths ... I will thrash and beat inside her and she will take and give ... enough for me to dissolve and crumble into her ... which I do willingly, painfully and lovingly ... she watches this event with a steady familiarity borne by untold millions of years genetically locked in some clue of memory... her eyes are full of this happening... she lazily watches the emptying of my eyes while far below and deep within her... fathoms deep... small forces are meeting the invaders... they will know what to do... they will harvest them... but only one will get through... he will give a message upon which is inscribed and in code, the secret of the universe.

Gross Intrusion

'Gross Intrusion' is the term used by auto-engineers when a car penetrates another causing death or injury to the occupant of the weaker car, whose body structure may have caved in too easily due to lack of what is called 'Structural Integrity'.

The guy poured some olive oil out of a bottle on to the palm of his hand, set the bottle down with his free hand and rubbed the olive oil first into both palms then onto his prick . . . then he casually and not before checking the nail of his index finger plunged the same finger into H's ass . . . took his finger out again as if satisfied with its location and pushed in his prick which entered slowly and gradually as the shocked sphincter was having to adjust its role from delivering to receiving. Slowly yielded the flesh and its co-ordinated network of fine muscles . . . they relaxed between moments of revulsion when all the sphincter wanted to do was to purge itself of the monster that was threatening it (what kind of turd is this?) and harness its forces to an almighty gesture of expulsion when the hole would resemble the iris of a camera at its smallest aperture, but each time the sphincter relaxed itself for a further intake of power that might crush the invader the cunning prick would advance further into his fleshy ranks. It was painful now as it made its inexorable journey against the natural grain of his tunnel ... it pushed, quelling any resistance, and each advance into his groin was followed by an almost involuntary withdrawal affording the active guy ecstasy since longitudinal rubbing and latitudinal squeezing is what petrassage is all about ... the push in needs to be followed almost immediately by a slow coursing out, as if having prepared the way by its initial attack the prick too withdraws to rally its forces to return and joyfully confirm its victory ... and so as not to lose ground the next movement in was even stronger in its thrusting power. For H, pain as it went in, and the incredible sensation as the prick withdrew, of shitting, plus the fear that he actually was, and half expected a strong smell of shit to come floating up to his nostrils. H was not familiar with these sensations which are part of the ecstasy of the passive recipient; that sense of possessing a cunt in one's ass, a strong centre of feeling whose payoff on being buggered is a sensation of shitting (the two, somehow, ineluctably combined). H was not yet refined in this more arcane pleasure of lovemaking, and to this end his curiosity became a seductive devil that tempted him to the present experiment. But this curiosity was born less out of the passion of the explorer than out of an evil growth that fed itself in the dank fields of waste and boredom and the desire to flagellate his skin and spirit into some sense of being alive ... and needed. This sense to be needed had perverted itself as it twisted away from its original course through lack of fulfilment, and careered blindly to another world ... any world where he could be of use. Or used. In normal times he would distribute his golden load one way only, disturbing and caressing a whole battery of nerves that clicked on, as the sphincter, like a chief electric nodule sensitised the area; and the charting of a torpedo-like turd to the lower depths was subtly and satisfyingly felt, right to its last tapering tail which reluctantly leaves, vacating the area that stretched and contracted for its expulsion, and as soon as it hit water the great lower intestine or ass-hole was already mourning its loss. Its loss of nag in the bum by the tenant that satisfies too. The ass was a normally dormant theatre compared to the sheer activity of the crazy twitchings in the tubes of flesh hanging and lolling in the front. But certain and gradual reversals were taking place . . . the desire dormant for so long was beginning to stir as if awaking from a long sleep. H would vaguely try to cast it back to oblivion but it had incubated for too long and wanted out. Who or what planted the seed one cannot here go into . . . suffice to say that it existed. H remembered those heaving and hot summer shits in the fields feeling the motions of almost burningly large turds coursing out of his system in the shape of men's pricks, so huge at times, even the size of pricks. Did that one come out of my tight little rosebud? He would simper to himself, occasionally delighting his skull's pornbox by gently inserting his little finger up his ass and feeling with wonder at how tightly even his little finger would be gripped, and thrillingly and frighteningly would conjecture how on earth the hard, large cocks of men would or could penetrate him. So, he would sit in the fields distantly gazing at the horizon with misty and soft-focused eyes, dim for pleasure . . . the pleasure of feeling so much in his hole. This new or gradually awaking discovery of an unexplored planet of delights within his being led him to fantasise about being taken unawares, as he sat there with naked loins, by an irate farm labourer and his mate who would be so incensed at the sight of H's naked joints that they would rudely throw him to the ground and slide their pricks up his still moist ass. In these moments H felt indeed like a quivering virgin. Now was reality ... now was the pain ... the guy was holding on to his prey like a terrier holds a rat, pushing deeper and deeper ... so deep it must be wounding me, H thought ... but he mustn't complain or shout out ... that would seem so silly. The man supported H under his belly pulling him up to encourage him onto his knees and almost making H impale himself on the stranger's weapon ... odd words came out from the man between quick hard breaths ... *'Hurt? You OK. ... Enjoying yourself cocksucker? ... Wan' it deeper? ... I'll fuck your head off!'* ... as passion grew inflamed, the stranger's text became more ribald and even ridiculous ... *'I'll kill you when I come you motherfucker! ... I'll eat you up you bastard!'* ... mixed with a reasonable variety of *'Ooohs'* and *'Heyssss'* and *'Haaaaaas'* ... *'Honey oh honey you make me feel so good!!!'* ... H said nothing but allowed it all, or rather submitted to it ... feelings now spent if they were ever there to spend ... sex sucked out of his being the way a raging fire sucks the oxygen out of a room ... as if sex had never existed except in his mind ... or in the fields with his little finger probing the little mouse of sensuality that had errantly taken lodging there ... or in the swollen bulges of men, in their nude swarthy flesh stiffening in the illicit camouflaging steam of Turkish baths, the haven of all the third sex. Now it was pain ... and yes, even now the acrid smell of shit came winging up as he crouched, beasted by a stranger now who fell for his erecting penis, fantasy-fed in the urinals of a favoured gay toilet and followed H, whose bait had hooked a monster that would not be easily assuaged by the little mouse. He followed, no words exchanged, just Harry's thumping heart led the way (the throb of fear not joy) to his room. And H sacrificed himself to the idea that at some point ecstasy would return and trade itself with this ridiculous fear ... and that as the stranger undid his flies and fire started to ignite his loins, it would continue and not abate ... but the size of him! ... it was a threat ... it was violent and would hurt ... H felt an unworthy combatant ... felt small and puny. The man was black and yes it was true ... it was no myth, since this one was indeed set like a donkey ... they do have vast quantities of cock ... and the small flame that lit a candle for H shrank away as the guy, without asking, took some oil off the shelf in the bathroom and poured it onto his hands like a gladiator oiling himself for the battle to the death ... or as if a complex operation was about to take place. He was priming his cock with a large palmful of oil, too much, but of course with that weapon how necessary! The black knew that his shaft needed bountiful lubrication and whereas a normal, hard and shrewd queen would have told him with no qualms where to get off in an act of self-preservation – what good is a stretched out queen? Harry could not. Harry was still shy in his exploration into the realm of his sexual identity. The black had said nothing but sensed his alarm and his fear ... was even used to guys freaking out over his tool and even turning on him, and he usually in those cases ended up with a blow-job or a friendly wank. He didn't mind which really, as long as he released a binful of spunk with a

whitey ... as long as he could be free in his
body ... and he sensed in Harry a victim but read
masochism in Harry's weakness where he should
have read simply fear ... the black was experi-
enced and gave value to what he read in men's
faces when their voices were too shy to betray
their deepest longings ... in this case he was
unaware that he was torturing H. How often do
you come across a gay in his thirties who is still a
virgin? As sex had removed itself from H it left
a dry room where nothing could grow (the black
senses the cold dry room deep within H and has no
desire to enter that particular abode). H's sexual
barometer remained flaccid ... and as the black
squeezed and pummelled H's hanging appendage
of skin, the emptiness of which drove the master
even further into his quest for pain, he seemed
determined to split poor H's intestines as an axe
splits oak. How dare whitey not be 'hard on' with
my beautiful black prick up his ass and half way
up his stomach, his renewed vigour seemed to
imply ... but H's hips ceased to move and just
presented themselves to the black like some
meagre sacrificial offering from a poor pagan to a
demon deity, as if to say that's all we have ... it's
not much, but it's living. *'Move, fuck you!! ...
move onto my prick!!'* He seemed to shriek at H's
dumb, prostrate white buttocks going gradually
red with impatient kneading ... Harry wobbled
uneasily on his knees and wanted to collapse onto
his stomach, but the black incensed now with the
strength that lust loans to muscles (no matter how
tired) to complete the act, held H up like a bag
of flesh and bones with his right arm and pulled
him onto the hilt where seemingly it could go no
further ... the black lifted his head and bared
his teeth like a donkey about to bray, arched his

back ... said ... 'OH FUCK FUCK FUCK
OOOH SHIT YOU FUCKER (what pain) OOH
FUUUCK YOU MOTHER YOU MOTHER
FUCKING COCKSUCKER ... I'LL EAT YOU
OOH MMMYY ... LICK MY SPUNK ... EAT
MY SHIT OOOH OOOH NOOO WOW WOW
WOWEE OH FUCK OH!! HONEY! NICE
NICE HONEY? CHRISTOFUCK!' The black
shuddered then fell down like a shot bull ... pant-
ing over H's back ... the weight of him collapsing
finally. H's precarious position ... dead feelings
crept into the proceedings ... the world seemed
to go very still and shadows would flit in and out
of H's eyes as if bats or even vultures were in the
room ... waiting ... numbness ... did not even
feel the shrinking of the black's penis as its spent
swill having whooshed into H was now returning
to the folds of peace ... a death smell lingered,
cold and dank around the prostrate limbs of the
victim which seemed to impersonate the spread-
eagled and twisted corpses of Auschwitz ... sleep:
H wanted sleep or to wrench himself free to throw
himself out of the window ... but most of all, what
the sane part of his mind wanted, wanted more
than anything else in the entire earth, was to
cradle in his arms a soft gentle woman, a soft
gentle and unfearful thing that had no pain ... no
threat ... no hard muscle or rough bristle ...
no vile hot stabbing greed investing him with
agony ... no scummy dirt or breath-stink-shit-
sour. Soft ... soft ... soft ... the word comforted;
talcum-powdered and tinkling voices ... soft
faces ... soft cheeks ... soft bosoms and rib-
bons ... innocent vulnerable thighs and always
soft, soft, soft downy brown ... his ass felt cold
and wet and even torn, as the organic compost
of shit, sperm and blood dripped its unsightly

mixture onto the sheets ... He was sick and weak and was sure some time had passed; feeling a heavy weight on him, the sleeping black. So H had drifted off ... had drifted off into a dream world peopled with the soft bodies, the sweet smelling bodies of women and woke to the shocking realisation of what the dead weight pinning him down was ... and with it came the burning, like corrosive acid, from his anus and the awful memory of the *thing* that felt as if still there, still undulating and thrusting and the black screaming invectives, the chorus for his excited secretions. Harry barely turned his head but could just see out of the corner of his eye a large red patch near his hips ... his or mine? But more than likely mine. He was circumcised and less likely to tear than a man who hadn't been. H felt sick and tearful and wanted the black growth like a burden from hell off of his back and out ... out for ever ... but H could only mutter ... 'Please ... Please ... would you get off me please ... please ... off me please ... do you hear?' *'Hallo sweetheart ... who's had a nappy then ... Hey! I must have had a shut eye ... Ha! Ha! Ha! nice one though, eh! Nice!'* As if the thought had encouraged him and the ghastly sleep refreshed him, H to his horror felt the man's slimy, sticky penis reswelling itself for the act. No, the black couldn't resume at this stage, must see how injured one of them was. 'No ... get off ... please, I'm ill.' But if fates worse than death had existed in H's imagination this must answer for the supreme ... once again he penetrated ... H attempted to twist away, though still on his belly, not on his knees ... *'Hold still cunt or I give it you!'* ... he took Harry's throat in his hands and gave a vicious but quick squeeze, as if to say how simple it would be for my powerful hands to snap this scrawny neck and how I hate your scrawny neck and what it's attached to but you must be obedient until I have had my fill ... H passed out for a second but had no doubt and read well messages of violence! They need no analysis and are not famous for innuendo. With his hands still holding onto his throat the black moved, gyrating like a dancer into the wound of the world ... Harry's poor torn sphincter ... he moved like he had all the time he needed and could indulge and savour as a gourmet whose first fierce hunger having been appeased, is able to relax and enjoy rather than satisfy ... 'please, please don't' ... a pathetic whine gurgled from his bloody mouth ... wherefore doth blood come into his mouth!!! Did he bite his tongue or did his heart burst!! The black heaved with a more spiky vigour ... *'On your knees ... Oh come on turd ... I'm nearly there ... Shit I nearly ... Nearly ... Come on ... I can't like this ... On your knees you fucker ... Come on mother ... Thaaats better ... Heeeeah ... Oh wow ... Hey thats wuuunderful ... Oh ... Oh ... Ohh!!!!! Ow Woow!'* The negro still held Harry by the throat and H was impaled to the hilt ... he was thrusting hard now and arched his back once more and as his moment of triumph came, bared his teeth, as if to holler it to the whole world ... did not of course see the blood seeping out of Harry's mouth nor feel the slackness when death calmly extinguishes the lights of a body ... OOW ... OW ... OW ... OW ... OW ... OW ... OW ... OW ... OH YEAH!!!!! YEAH!!!! OOOOOOOOOH!

False God

Alone in the room ... all alone and silent with nothing and no one ... his sex locked away in a vault bound with manacles of fear ... rusting and petrifying into the cold iron ... alone ... feeling only a warm drowsiness induced by the spluttering gas fire ... cold on the inside warm on the outside ... growing older by the minute ... The strands of taut life slackening ... a life that had thrust him through a thousand orifices ... hard as a chain that drives a machine, oiled and lubricated, the force of his drive was once as strong as a new two-stroke engine, his thrust was as rapid, and his viscous explosions were once an unending source of pleasure to the thousand or so women he estimated he had splattered his silken jets into ... A seemingly limitless supply, a cornucopia of spunk seemed to be his mass of flesh, unending until death, a perennial bloom, with each valve and tissue, vein and artery conjoining in a holy alliance to produce in his sacs the vital DNA. The Sting ... the magic paste to weld life together, cell by molecular cell, sewn by a host of minute fairies. He would aim his swollen tool into warm, pulsating, rubbery caves whose owners squealed at the new tenant's occupation of their many and multifarious rooms. He had wanted to populate the world ... to cram into those blind and, to him,

screaming hungry mouths, his generous flesh, to
be an unending supply to an unending demand,
to satisfy and fulfil the hunger of the female
human race . . . his ambition had been this fuelled
by such motives . . . as if nothing else in life that
he had seen or felt capable of was worth achieving,
since it was all so vapid and ephemeral. No career
could compensate for the time it stole from your
youth; for the time it snatched from the need and
act of love . . . and it not only stole time but sapped
the flower and drained the perfume, as some youth
with bent spine hung his head into musty tomes
resembling nothing more than a wilting
daffodil . . . these intellectual eunuchs with their
seldom exercised shafts of cocooned flesh . . . only
books they produced or symphonies to amuse the
masses or to distract them from their own need
to be fulfilled . . . nodding their heads in some vast
sterile palace of culture to the frenzied baton of a
geriatric whilst their brains were swarming with
distracted dreams of lubric pleasures. The vagina
and penis would create their own symphonic
variations . . . he knew for certain that his baton
could excite more than anything else in the world's
treasure house of sensations . . . No woman could
be possessed by anything more powerful and
amazing than a sizeable hunk of mankind stirring
up between her thighs a froth of gore-dew whilst
disturbing her mind with sexual dramas as intense
as Shakespeare's sonnets. So, his ascent into the
world of sex had been swift and prodigious, he
had taken all he could and gave always more.
He had drained himself like a river until the sedi-
ments and rocks were exposed, yet he would be
refilled again as if by the omnipotent ocean . . .
filled . . . blown up with a riot of blood called by
the brain into action. And they truly loved him

for it ... he gave to many and refused none ... was a Jesus dividing his loaf among the multitudes and the more he gave the greater seemed his capacity. Everyone had their fill and few complained although some demanded of him the sacrifice of totality to themselves ... that he break his rock only into them, had not understood his mission which was to all, a calling from the Most High who had instilled in him this God-like capacity. They had been gently dealt with though sometimes furious scenes ensued as if the sacrifice of their bellies demanded the life-long enchaining of the beast that fed them. But this animal must hunt like the lion and the wolf and no one enchains them ... must have many litters and enlarge the scope of nature since God, Pan or Zeus had created him for this role ... his sap must feed mankind and create much fruit ... a rich harvest lay in his rotund balls and as she guided his prick into her belly his eyes closed with the familiar feeling of home and on opening them gazed on the many different expressions on their faces ... as he ground his pestle into her mortar, undulating it as if to explore every corner of a new continent, their faces would take on the expressions of Greek tragic masks, so caught were the features into themselves. They might look pained but were concentrating on catching the visions that soar up like multicoloured birds of paradise disturbed from their sleep in the dense foliage ... swam in oceans of sensations as his stack choked them and for others it dislodged the dust from the walls and broke the crust of neglect and light poured into their wombs as into a long neglected tomb and they came to life again as their lips wept hot unguents and a myriad of tremors shook their continents and rivers swelled

their banks and fish poured upstream to lay their
eggs and then he would leave, withdraw only after
a long and supreme effort . . . when his exploration
had exposed every part that was capable of exploration. Constant fucking removed the fear of
premature ejaculation and whilst he would enjoy
it more and savour and relish the delights, his
gates to the dam would remain obdurately
closed . . . until the right moment when she would
come, dissolve and flow downstream, after the
rages of the falls and rapids had tossed her into
madness . . . The peaceful aftermath when floating
gently in her own liquids . . . he'd unleash his quiet
load of spunk . . . note the prick jerk and rear its
head, pulse out its last exclamations and be still . . .
a dead thing, slain. To come before her would be
anathema to him, would pull him back to the
earth before he left the gravitational field, would
plummet him down to be impaled upon a savage
cliff, helpless like Prometheus, blown by icy
winds . . . not melting in a volcano that he had
made erupt or hurtling to the stars, but impotent
and marooned, scummed by his own seed . . . but
thought he, 'Good' . . . another target, another
sacrifice to his altar where the pudenda were worshipped as the cradle of life . . . not lifeless stone
or remote deity, or preaching celibate or ghostly
historical ascetic or dead words in cracked and
dusty books, but alive . . . there . . . now . . . he
worshipped the Mary of her cunt. All cunt was
holy and all screamed aloud for blessing . . . his
duty and his prayers were to the filling and blessing of it . . . cunt is the Temple of God and is the
cradle of life and God fills the orifice with his
presence and enters his prick too since the God
Head is a twin deity . . . and no cunt is ever different from another cunt except as a face is different,

since at the moment that the Almighty enters and illuminates his altar he shows his face to be there, smiling with the savage grin of a satyr ... but God will only enter the cunt at that moment when it becomes alive and flowers and is filled, for only then will He give his blessing. Thus am I a religious being, a devout priest ... a holy Man of God ... his saint on earth and verily do I worship at God's chosen temples within whose walls I offer myself up to him ... 'Hear Oh Ye Kings, Give Ear Oh Ye Princes, I, Even I Will Sing Unto the Lord' ... and people came from far and wide to genuflect at his altar of Priapus and his beneficent, swollen-cheeked, roseate God winked down at his High Priest's devotion and blessed his flesh and urged it on to greater and greater feats and fine webs of skin were formed in countless soft caves catching and weaving miracles of the aftermath that he set in motion ... Some alas did not bear fruit and some were viciously cast out into the night by violent hands in brilliantly lit chambers of horror, where gleamed sharp and relentless scalpels in whose reflection moved convex shapes in white, like stealthy murdering ghosts ... these others did not want the host planted there since many liked only the digging and the rooting, therefore much sinew and fine membrane became a feast for the sewer rats or was burned at terrible sacrifices ... and these events caused in him terrible pangs of guilt and sleepless nights when he would suddenly awake, alone and, through custom, forgetting for the moment that he was alone and unsuccessful that day, turn over to grasp for comfort the warm woman that was usually there ... but she wasn't and he'd clasp his own empty space and knot his grey sheets in his fists and moan into his seamy pillow and bewail that dozens of women were

alone too, many hundreds and yet here he
was . . . alone, and the thought of them lying likewise alone and needing him plunged him into even
greater confusion . . . or else they were with other
men . . . others were clasping the flesh he so much
needed now . . . others grinding their hips and
tying their tongues into wet knots . . . and she was
admiring some man and being bathed in the seat
of his effort but not him! . . . And she was opening
her eyes in wonder as the man was stabbing her
groin with his vile sceptre, and screaming as she
came, but not for him that sweet sound . . . and
from all over the city he imagined the wails of
fornication issuing from the mouths of thousands
upon thousands, and the rivers of spunk that must
be flowing that night or any night, but not his, and
imagined the moaning of their voices rising in
unison like sirens to torment him and strained his
ears and seemed to catch the sound floating on
the wind . . . And the thought burned into his temples and he mourned as for a dead one, wailed
why wasn't she here . . . any she, since they are all
the same . . . all of them . . . different only in the
size of shoes or taste in music or degree of sugar
in their coffee and yes they liked to think each
one was so different from the other, so unique, so
special, unlike any other creature in the world
but when God entered their bodies they became
HIM . . . God-struck . . . 'and I am faithful only to
him whose presence in the flesh I communicate
with . . . I fuck for God's sake!' But wasn't God
manifested in other flesh, those others that were
entwined like honeysuckle twisting in and out of
the dark sleeping streets and shuttered windows,
whilst he lay empty and aching. Was he not there
in the bodies of others that performed as he did?
But he could not conceive that He was there in

the true spirit as He was in him . . . in me exists the
world . . . outside me lives nothing . . . outside of
me nothing exists but for the fact that I perceive
it in my own mind . . . in my mind exists the
universe . . . cut out my mind and it ceases to be.
Therefore God can exist only for me. I cannot feel
my cock in some other man's cock or feel her cunt
being stabbed by him . . . I can only know it, and
knowing it hurts . . . Then in torments of anguish
did he fitfully sleep in a bed, slimy and
unkempt . . . in a room with a stove to one side
and some half-eaten, takeaway chop suey that was
congealing in a paper carton on the sideboard . . .
An ashtray filled with butt-ends like dead locusts
and a sink next to the stove filled with dirty week-
old crockery. And he grew worse as his desperation to worship God increased and in increasing,
the intensity of his search frightened off those
whom the gods themselves imbue with their spirit
and they sought new altars. One winter H surveyed his dim eye on the glass and with his finger-
tips adjusted his receding greying hair, turned on
the gas fire and so felt warm again. He sat in the
chair feeling drowsy but not wracked by walking
the streets and searching cafés for the lonely that
he'd try to induce to his now threadbare feast . . .
God, thought H, was deserting him now and even
his limp flesh felt stringy as though by no power
could this flaccid thing ever be metamorphosed
into the instrument it once had been. God has
deserted me . . . Or else did I worship false
gods? . . . No . . . Perhaps, H mused, it was a pun-
ishment, a chastisement for the lives of the innocent and unborn that were sent back to him
unclaimed . . . Thereafter, when many moons had
driven the seed of life through millions of women
and autumn had once again paraded past his

windows flecked in the riotous colours of nature
dazzled by its own life force, he decided that what
he needed to fulfil God's wishes was a wife . . . To
share the seasons and witness the glow of life
illume her each month and bear the fruit of his
seed and feel the ebbs and flows of her tides. In
this way would he make amends and expiate any
sin he might have unconsciously committed in his
zealous worshipping. He would worship God
anew, and so he looked, and no one looked more
fiercely or committed themselves with such
ardour, but somehow he felt that time was out of
joint for him and even the approaching of a female
was now so painful in anticipation of rejection that
his courage would fail. He prayed to God but his
prayers were evidently not heard and he remained
alone in his room with the gas fire. But as chance
will have it, what is suited to you will sense your
need or you will eventually sense it, and be led to
your goal. So he found himself one day, just as
spring was beginning to nudge the merest swelling
in the buds and the cherry blossoms were sending
dizzy-eyed creatures silly with joy, found himself
in a seedy area of the city near the commercial
section, having finished his shift as a night-porter
in a third-class hotel . . . there, in a shop window,
was a sight that caught his eye and fuelled his
imagination and not without some pangs of lust.
She was pretty . . . nay even beautiful, and stared
back at him with that ever-so-slightly haughty
glance that interested women adopt as if to veil
their true inclination. He went inside the shop . . .
The first time that he ever dreamed of going into
one of those places having hitherto no need of
them, and very quietly asked the assistant who
was a rather sympathetic lady how much it was . . .
and pointed since he could not frame the words,

to the inflatable woman in the window... After, and in the confines of his room, he found that although she wasn't his ideal she nevertheless was extremely sweet and was indeed built such as the manufacturers guaranteed... It was quite incredible and when a shiver of life reignited his member with the current that had for so long been absent he climbed aboard the plastic replica and wept to God for at last forgiving him and worshipped him at his new shrine... holding his wife in his arms he poured sweet nothings into her ear and swore eternal devotion... she smiled mysteriously and numbly back.

North

DAY ONE

Got on my bike – Homer and Ulysses beckon
whenever I am kissed and licked by the sun. Drove
to the end of the road, seas hard and painful bright
blue. Clouds are dappled grey, sinews creep out
darkening the sea – seaweed in long tapering
fingers in the shallow emerald green. Sky fresh
now as washed linen, clouds, puffy mashed potato,
fields thick with rolling spinach, cascading down
like liquid velvet or paint, or paint running and
smudging – streaked! A bramble, a tree trunk hits
the eye as the eye-radar swirls and scans around
the skull. Stop the bike, it steams like a marathon
runner; walk, spreading thicket; God, foot in
stream, in rut, in swamp, in marsh, squelch and
onwards. Me, chest hard, heaving, breathing,
smelling the odour of ordure, a slush of fresh-
baked dung newly – damn! – broken by my blind
foot; misplaced, the dung is fresh again, shiny.
Wool on wire – wind stops, and for a second the
world hangs silent. Eyes scan into the distant
receding vista witnessing there in the middle of
my vision a sail cutting the loch, two birds swoop
on something – looking like hawks as they do,
silhouette black against the sky they cut a piece
out and wheel out of sight. Up, spore marks in

the sky, whispered secrets, white moustaches. Then the wind blows that sound again, really a sighing of mourners in a large echoing cathedral at Cologne. Breath snatched from the trees, air, sea, loch. Its taste is stored and expelled, big shadows on the hills move slowly, you know, like stains, sweat stains which move – dark patches. The sheep scatter in quick steps at your approach. Sun high and cold, gleaming with snatches of windless heat. The loch and hills fade into the disappearing apex of your vision as a primitive timeless landscape. Your bike gleams and cools and waits. It moves you more easily than you move yourself. You sit and it moves, you turn a handle and it thrusts immediately between your legs, shivers, and bundles of power and cool air refreshes. It waits, your steel servant, steel and spoked rubber. For now you would rather be under the sun-baked heather dung-stung air, sea-choked and weed-filtered peat of centuries, than your machine. A beetle hurtles to the underworld in a peaty stream trapped into stagnancy by a receding tide. With some weed, and blocking his entrance, the beetle dives and wiggles aimlessly and then comes up for air in little wiggly jerky movements. The loch turns to the blue of outer-space pure where it deepens into cerulean and violet. Dusk, the stars are thrown across the sky as if handfuls of seed fixed into the black, cold, sharp needle-points staring down at the scene, star-tracks scorch home through the ether burning nocturnal emission; a sliver of white, a luminous bow, Cupid's arrow, a bit of dust, 'Oh look, a shooting star!' It disappears as fast.

Sleep.

DAY TWO

The sun scorches on the neck, the boats are frozen in a lake of tears; memory waves beckon and soften the determination of the spine. A sparrow hovers over a spider in a clump of grass, fluttering in space not moving only airborne, wing-tips, neck bent down resembling an upturned trembling hook.

I saw swans in the lake that was still as a mirror, throwing the sky's face back. The swans idled out as alabaster carvings. The breakfast was nice, the tea drained through the plumbing and squashed and mashed the eggs. Slept fitfully, tossing and turning, trying to find the right cipher in my bed, the right symbol that would bring peace to my twisted body, curled, stretched. Oh for sleep, oh the rage in the guts. The laughter from the other rooms, let me get drunk oh Lord, let me thrive in the wreckless abandonment of my senses, let me career aimlessly and thoughtlessly with outsize voice and slither through emotional visceral lakes where dams have been broken, and it all gets mixed up. Let me touch on madness and giggle furiously in the ridiculous quivering spectacle of myself turning into a mass of wobbling joy. Oh the control, let me let it go, let me be free – to sing and scream and howl, reaching down into my stomach with trowels and bulldozers to smash and excavate the hardened and constipated life stuck to the walls, burn it off, shudder and explode into life.

DAY THREE

Breathless I was – aghast! Gulping for air, steadfast on my machine, I was hurled 200 miles, stopping to refuel on the awful main-road tourist route, the ghastly coaches lined with waxed portraits staring out of stale bodies (or rather containers). Oh, oh, oh my God ... The hills move as I zip through them. They curl around me and wave and slip a few valleys in, gorges and passes (yes). Or rise higher and higher and slither down in loose rock sediment, chippings and silt, and sometimes the hills astride, I hurtle through them; they wait for me, inviting me to skim through the centre, what's on the horizon? Unravelled mantles of ochre and sea-green, and up spun a dove and then a starling swept across me. A swift, a swallow. Did it dive down – did it disappear – tears in the windgripped eyes – the wild windswept eighty mph, and choked blast cut and slashed, cold fingers of ice play softly on your face. Oh the sun aches and twists, bulges, and seems ready to burst. Oh it changes colour now, tries on a gown or 'whose party, darling will this do?' Black thin trees splatter the space and cut, tattoo themselves over the sun's belly. She looks well tonight – it heaves itself out of the forest dragging tangles of branches; it's dark, it vomits out of the mountain like the birth of Apollo, trailing nerve endings it hides and the cool dull wind, sad wind, chastens and it's lonely without the warm-hearted red rotund bursting cherry-big scorched friend who hides, oh she peeks out now, sends out long piercing stalks of light; she's there. Tin lines – lines of tin-crushed auto-spectators move in a line down the road. Four bikes overtake me; bikes overtaking undoubtedly wave. Facing opposite directions,

zoning towards each other at combined speeds of
160 mph they will usually, not always, but usually
flash their front-light, but in passing may wave.
These do, the long line of tin cars is oppressive,
they move like a sick and dying caterpillar crawling for a space to expire. The other cars, now a
longer space. Is there room ahead, flash frequently
but not frequently enough – not to risk overtaking.
A narrow road, you see, full of bends! Quite a
few hills, no direct view for seventy-five yards so
you overtake quickly and suddenly if you see just
a bit of space then are swallowed back into the
stream allowing the on-coming cars their space,
since they bring towards you, in the opposite
direction, a half-ton of power fast enough to hurl
you into vertical ascent if you do not side-step
quickly enough. There are blind bends, blind hills,
blind but carrying a certain sense of death. You
join the tin necklace, are you the jewel in
between? They lie sunken in their seats in front,
you imagine the chat, the kiddies climb over the
seat. Some artificial thing, revolting, waves its
head, sitting in the back-rest, it waves its head like
an insane creature on the back-seat, it waves its
head with red eyes. Clouds gather at the corner
of the frame and the wind reverses into your chest;
flies meet your goggles with squelchy embraces, a
little farmhouse – shall we live there dear? Grinding out corn and wheat – baking our own bread.
Where dear? It's gone. It's now a waterfall. Where
dear? It's gone. It's now a field. Where? It's gone
– it's gone – a horse, a clump of trees, an empty
space, a streak of green, zoom! zoom! two cars,
now a longer space. Is there room ahead, flash on
my winker, right hand, and open up the throttle.
It starts, it easily overtakes. Good, there's space
ahead, enough in case another car in front has

pulled out too, so safe if not for him for me, but no – he pulls sharply, returns to the womb from whence he came. He returns, just sneaking back into the space he left and leaving me to face, in the distance, that from which he withdrew. At the speed of light, the opponent's lights snap on, warning me he can go nowhere. On his left a steep incline, behind others hurtling too fast for sudden decision – so hell, I pull out all my stops to overtake, just one small metal cylinder of flesh packed with sweat, pock-marked, fag-choked. I have just fifty yards at least but oh why doesn't it overtake? I stay the same; ahead he's blinking at me. Twenty-five yards, why will my bike not sweep up and overtake? The monster on my left with grin and piss-off chortle speeding out to stop me, will not drop back – prevents my returning to the fold. He's increased his speed to keep me on the right lane. I drop behind but my space is taken by another; he's alarm-filled, quick I turn and see his panic. He's moved up but behind him others have moved up too – the lump of screaming tin still speeds forbidding me to overtake. I scrape so close to him we might be twins, the scum and filthy seated piece of human flesh afraid now in case I come too close, breaks now to let me in. Oh God, too late, too late . . . The roaring ton ahead with open maw is on me, eyes turn to water, heart to milk, it's there, it grows . . . scream.

ONE SECOND LATER

With the ripening corn, small and shiny black things wriggle under the sun and spinners plait and weave under brambles overgrown for the season. Cloudless now, blue hot scorched tight moodless

stretched sheet of sky so fine and the earth has
been scraped and the peat, funnelled and turned
for small trees growing – pines – forests will come.
The giant eagles claw the skies at Ardnamurchan
in Ballachulish – the sun throws millions of lights
into the loch and the dead sleep in the churchyard
peacefully. Somewhere from above a deluge of
rain – in red? Imagine it slowly and dreamily, like
an ice-flow breaking up in the spring solstice. The
screeching – the screaming of brakes, hand and
foot squeezing, pushing down, passenger ahead
flying through dashboard window as if diving into
pools on razor-clear August mornings. The glass
shimmers and dissolves on impact like splashing
water – mixed with (the passenger this) a detached
vein here – by itself, located in the neck –
unhooked from home by a clever sliver of glass
left from a mid-air split-second-time, stopped-
shutter-frozen leap – then continue, the vein
moving like an agitated worm searching – blind
worm being born alive by the power of the flow
that cascades freely out, the oil tank that cracked
and dripping – rent body of the car from the gross
intrusion (how dare you) of another car up its rear
end – piercing and foully penetrating – oiled and
splutter – shatter. Body of one, the swallow-diver
on the tarmac – fountain still on – the driver
biting on the wheel – his teeth, sprung out or
buried bits in lips, redistributed you might say. But
in any case saved by the wheel which only cracked
a rib or two, nudging the curved bone of his ribs
into the lung – only (oh go on!). But the petrol –
oil and blood mix (not well) on the tarmac. It's
hot now we've stopped, so hot the bike – mine –
had simply annihilated itself. Its front became a
ragout of rubber, spokes and steel and separated
from the rest, as if it had been shaved off – close!

The rest just melted (as if) twisted by an angry mighty fist . . . and you 'describe what you saw'. I saw the sky rise up and the earth recede below. I travelled high above the vile throng as if thrown and witnessed a lake I had not seen before from the ground but up it shone as bright as silver from my vantage point in space, as bright as a dollar, and small figures were gathered at its edge with fishing rods, standing very still and calm, and still the valley moved across my eyes. A plane murmured high, leaving a thin small mark in the impervious blue and far below I witnessed the snake had stopped, bunching up into its centre and then finally quiet. At the point of impact dense segments growing wider towards the tail and the faces staring out red; this one with blotch and tape over the nose, face out, hand over mouth like this, straining to see, breast heaving in a marzipan orange low-cut Marks and Sparks sweater with kiddie-winks crawling over. 'Get down Richard.' 'Oh let me see mum!' Whacks and looks, eyes grovelling and hungry for bits of flesh that should be attached, horror-hungry. 'Oh did you' – she says, blonde short-bobbed hair, large teeth, voice a gurgle with orgasmic excitement, throat opened and released – 'Did you . . . see it?' Ooooooh it was – he just – that car!! It was ooooooh!' Sibilant and gleaming teeth with piece of gum stacked in the corner of the mouth for future use. The scene slowly moves but imperceptibly, not that you'd notice really – flying in space, the azure deepening to purple, the trees racing together – melting as one; the river turned to a thin line or scar or spit-gleam tracing its way into the distance and the loch to a half-dollar piece, the tin snake is still in heat-sweat – the kids are crying and the road is smeared with its compost of oil, blood and the

114

shit that flew out of the combatants. Glass and wire of human and machine entangle. Burn.

TWO MINUTES LATER

I was hurled amongst the stars, thrown by an almighty power and tossed into the deep of painless space, vacuumed into oblivion and into velvet layers I entrust myself. My body's turned to ash, my skin to molecules, my eyes to atoms, my blood to neutrons; then spun into space my disembodied atoms resemble a galaxy – a universe of stars – I spread as I travel speed of light years ahead. The atoms drift apart leaving so much space between each one, but not lost. From the edge of the universe, from there, I still resemble – still look like me but close to I'm just a mass of space and emptiness but the thoughts are whistling transmogrified into energy and waves lassoing the universe, lassoing the planet. Earth hallo, can you hear me? They're waking up in San Francisco, to bed in Shoreditch. Later. Where is he? she wonders, throwing the cat out and bolting the door. He's late. Late? (Bone splintered, eyes burst open by shock.) She puts the milk-bottle out (an arm is severed, lying in a field of corn; she loved that arm stroking her so finely). She turns on the reading light, looked forward to him strong and young in his years, he strides over them not weighed down – where's the sound of his bike, he should be back by now. Her ears alert, tentacles taut, eyes wide for every bike that comes down the street, but recognising the chortle throb. No, not that one, no not that, where is he now, he's late. Dinner-heating, cat scratching at window (invisible angels flutter over the sight of hell with

puckered mouths, hands clasped to head like old
rabbis, gestures of shrug and is there any hope?)
'Did you see it?' Slowly. 'Be a witness.' Whilst he
flies into the third circle of the universe, the world
now is spirit-lamp-lit one side. She's gone to bed.
Oh come on, cuddle and stroke and I'll put my
knees behind you like chairs. His wife is soft –
your limbs are dismembered. Imagine yourself
with her, the ticking of the clock, your hand on her
hip, resting gently as if . . . only hear her breathing.
Don't place yourself there now – unstitched skin
is horrible, disorganised, not nice. A caterpillar
slides over a leaf, buckling up and crawling out
again, head in the air twitching like a metronome,
undecided, settles eventually to nibble on the edge
of the leaf, mandibles working furiously, the leaf
disappears slowly resembling a sieve – now what
does it think as its shining black head pours over
its salad? Back to the scene. Oh he's hurt, the one
with the plaster nose-protector uttered, don't look
Ethel – grunts fat and sloppy with a battered hat,
don't look for God's sake, there's tiny dewdrops
of blood on the windscreen and we're six cars
back – ugh! Get a cloth, wipe the windscreen for
Christ's sake, it's dry Bert, it's dry, it just makes a
smear! Ohhh! All that was inside him and now
it's on the windscreen. Your husband is on the
windscreen. Just wipe it off Ethel! Wipe me off –
what constitutes me? My blood – my organised
body, broken, am I still me? But it's dry! So spit
on it Ethel, do it – oh for fucks sake! You do it!
Don't say that in front of the – fuck it, just give
it to me, I'll do it. A spiral of sanguine red spun
out under the sun, sprayed the crops, anointed the
road, slimed the cars, freckled the windows, dyed
his clothes, fed the flies, and he was in the blood
as the blood was in him before he took off for

other worlds. But blood held the passion together, pasted the thoughts and fed the motor, drove the piston and filled his organ for acts of riot and spell and magic at carnivals of flesh where now no more will he create the future world, now it lay defeated as a thousand dreams and anguished moans lay shattered with it. Witness the pretty faces flying out of his mind as he leaves this world – see his life flying past him with small soft faces embedded as jewels in a bracelet of his thought, or raisins in a cake – childlike faces fringed with tassles of downy hair. Choose one. The rain starts to fall. He'll be wet. He'll come in soaking and cold with his knees and thighs drenched through; the afternoon was so hot the cat slept in the shadow of the dustbin. His cottage-cheese in the fridge, a light is on in the hall. A salad sits greenly in a bowl, dressing in a little cup. There is a nice new silky nightie, an old Victorian slinky silky nightie that holds my body in its warmth, as if it were holding something precious. The tick of the gas-meter breaks the silence. Is that a key in the lock? He's come, footsteps perhaps? The world turned yellow, red, then a whitish blue and I joined a swarm like bees or atoms like a cloud of locusts, and we, this cloud and me, moved together, each particle attracting the other, each neutron circling around in its own energy-field and they held me within them and feeling no fear I soared and was happy to be part of this radiant universe, and colours fractured and melted, changed and prismatised, violet sunk into vermilion and became scorched magenta. Worlds drifted past in smelting gaseous glows which always looked so solid.